DOUBLE DESTINY

SHADOWS OVER ELISTA, BOOK 5

CLARA WILS

Gryphon's Gate Publishing

Double Destiny

Copyright © 2022 Clara Wils

Gryphon's Gate Publishing
550 King St. N.
PO Box 42088 Conestoga
Waterloo, ON
N2L 6K5

Print ISBN: 978-1-990587-19-1

CHAPTER 1

ROO

"No!" I screamed, lurching up to a sudden and horrible wakefulness. I didn't know how I knew, but Dawn was dead.

I'd felt it.

We were deeply linked. She'd reaffirmed that only yesterday. I'd felt our connection as well, when she'd reached through it to touch my spirit. But I hadn't known until now, how intimately I had felt her presence; not until... it was gone. "Dawn, no," I whimpered.

"What happened?" Falcon asked from the other side of the room. He and Rhino were trying their best to bandage each other's wounds. Ceph had been tended to and now lay on the floor, barely breathing. My own stomach wound had been bound with strips torn from the bottom of my dress. I blinked as I took this all in.

"Dawn?" Rhino asked.

"I... I can feel..." I trailed off. It was odd. I knew she

was dead — I felt that as a certainty — and yet... I still felt something from her.

Had some part of her survived? *Dawn?* I sought out through our connection. I'd been able to speak with her this way earlier that same day.

Roo? Is that you? How...? Dawn's voice was strong in my mind.

I felt your death, I said softly.

I... I'm sorry, I killed Swan, but she took me with her. But... There was something odd in Dawn's voice. *I am still... aware of things? How can this be?*

It's your spirit, young one. This was a new voice I didn't recognize.

Amya? What do you mean? Dawn asked. Ah... so the new voice was Dawn's Lumani, the spirit dwelling within her. But... how had I been able to hear it?

"Roo? What's going on?" Falcon asked again.

I raised my hand to forestall any other questions. I needed to listen. I didn't know how long I'd be in contact with Dawn before her spirit fled this world.

Amya continued: *You've always been strong in spirit, stronger than any I've ever known. And when you took Swan's spirit, you bolstered your own. I... I don't know what's happened, but if you were truly dead, I'd have returned to the Mists. I... I think your spirit is strong enough that it is... lingering.*

For how long? Dawn asked.

I don't know, this is new to me.

Is there anything we can do? I can do? I asked.

There may be, yes. I was a little surprised at Leoa commenting on this. Apparently, my own Lumani spirit had heard everything.

Leoa, is that you? Amya asked, amazed.

Yes, Amya, it's me. And I think there is a way Roo and I can save you and Dawn.

I'm all ears... or all spirit... all spirit ears? Dawn joked. I smiled, not quite believing she could jest at a time like this. That was Dawn for you.

Can you find us? Leoa asked. *We're in the village. Come to us. Roo, you'll need to accept Dawn and Amya into yourself the same way you accepted me. I know our Bond took weeks to form, but we don't have that sort of time. I'm hoping you can Bond with Dawn and Amya and host them inside of you. Once they have a body again, I don't think they will dwindle and fade.*

You may be right. That could work, Amya said. *We're coming.*

Dawn and I are already bonded, I said, knowing it was true. *I do not think this will be difficult.*

They arrived quickly. I couldn't see them... not truly, though I felt their presence through my spirit-gift, I felt their emotions, their soul. And perhaps because of that, I thought I saw just a hint of hazy colors nearby: fiery reds and oranges, the colors of Dawn's spirit.

I adjusted myself to a kneeling position, sitting upon my legs, and found — difficult as it was with all that had happened today — a place of calm within me.

Leoa helped. *Yes, find your core, your spirit. See the link to your sister, your beloved. Accept them into you, Bond with them.*

"Dawn and Amya, I know you are here with me." I spoke the words aloud like a ritual, but echoed them inwardly as well. "I can feel you, as... as I think I have always felt you." I held out my arms to them, even though I didn't need to, what I was doing was an act of spirit, not of flesh and bone. "Come to me, my sister, my heart, my twin spirit," I said, and I felt the nearness of Dawn and Amya, like a heavy, damp heat all around me. Their spirit pressed upon me.

Dawn, connect to me, like you did yesterday, through our link. And I will pull you into me and Bond with you.

Yes, Roo. I... I love you, my twin spirit, she breathed softly. I felt the emotion in her voice. *Thank you!* Then I felt her connect, felt her pull on that same part of me I'd felt yesterday. I too connected with her through that link and suddenly Dawn was there, standing before me. She looked as she had in life, though her form was translucent, ephemeral. She smiled.

I rose from my kneeling position and put a hand to her cheek, feeling its warmth, even though there was no true flesh where I touched, just spirit.

"I accept you into me," I whispered, bundling that spirit form in my arms, holding her close and then pushing her closer still, within me, Binding her to me.

Ohhhhh, Dawn said softly as it happened. Her voice went from being a distant echo, to clear as day as it came to be fully within me, bound to my spirit, four souls in one body.

For just a moment, I didn't have control of myself, Dawn did. She reached with my hands to run them over my body.

You're so... big and... full and... She laughed. *And welcoming. No wonder our guys can't get enough of you. This body is amazing!*

I laughed a little as Dawn's control faded and I was myself again. I didn't know what to say to that, but she knew how I felt; that I was just happy she was alive.

This is it, Amya said softly. *We are one.* And in that moment, I felt something else, a second merging of spirit.

I nearly wept at the love and devotion and caring and desire which blossomed within me as Amya and Leoa merged — just for a moment — into one. I recalled that they had been lovers in previous lives. I was happy Dawn and I could bring them together once again. Their love was so pure and invigorating I lost track of time, basking in its radiant glow.

"Roo?" It was Swift's voice, as his strong arms enfolded me. "What's... happening? The others said you were talking to Dawn, like she was here?" He was concerned.

I blinked, returning to myself and seeing the room again. I turned to Swift and with — what must have been a beatific smile — I said, "I... no, Dawn... lost her body, but her spirit is within me now; her and her Lumani. All of us."

Then, the extremity of what I'd just done caught up to me and my exhausted body. I felt darkness swirl around me as fatigue claimed me. The last thing I recalled was Swift catching me as I fainted.

But it didn't matter. I could rest now.

The battle was done, and Dawn was safe within me.

Thank you, sister.

Thank you, beloved.

I didn't know which of us said each of those. I just rejoiced that my dearest companion was still with me, beyond death. I let myself float in this darkness, giving myself time to recover, so I could find out more about this strange and wonderful new Bond I'd formed.

CHAPTER 2

RHINO

"Is she well?" Falcon asked.

Swift was setting Roo down softly to the floor. "I think she just fainted. She's breathing well and her pulse is strong." He knelt next to her, looking at her for a long moment before looking at us. "I... only just got here, did what she say make sense to anyone else?"

"I'm too tired and hurt to make sense of anything. I have no clue what just happened," I said, laying back and trying not to move. My myriad injuries didn't hurt quite as much if I could just lay still. I hoped that healer from Elista got here soon.

Did it make sense to you? I asked Iomu?

Nope, sorry.

I gave up and just rested.

"Swift, are the enemy dealt with?" Falcon asked. He too sounded as tired and injured as I did.

"Yes. There aren't many of us left, but there are enough to start gathering up the enemy. The Thraians are starting to come around, but they can clearly see their dragon is dead and ours is still flying over the town. The fight seems to have gone out of them. They aren't surrendering exactly, but they're not fighting either." Swift rose and went to the window. "It's... just a big mess out there."

And in here.

And everywhere.

Oh... but it had been a glorious battle. After having been beaten down by the dragon lord in the last fight, I had proven myself this time. I'd had fifty men with me, and we'd made the enemy pay dearly for each one of ours who'd fallen. I couldn't say exactly, but I guessed we'd taken down fifty of the enemy for each of ours. I smiled with grim satisfaction.

Then I passed out.

I roused, feeling an intense and uncomfortable warmth all over me. Through bleary eyes I looked up to see that same healer from earlier, hands upon me, smiling down.

"Just relax," they said. I realized the warmth was only where I'd been injured. It was just that I had so many wounds, it felt like it was everywhere. Still, I was too exhausted to do anything other than comply with their words and rest.

I felt my heat rise, a fever coming over me, then... I think I slept for some time after that. I woke from time to time, delirious and sore. I'd roll over only to cause shooting pain, which would wake me. I'd opened a wound, which had been starting to scab over. That went on for a while. Then I moved on to waking to an incredible itch all over, and learned quickly not to scratch, as that could take off a scab as well.

When I finally woke feeling mostly... normal, I found myself in a bed, glorious light streaming in the window of the small room I occupied. I tested movements slowly and carefully, finding my body responding well, with minimal pain. I was still covered in bandages, but I felt compelled to rise and sit on the edge of the bed. Curious, I unwound some of the bandages to see the state of my injuries. A few bits of scab came away painlessly with the cloth to reveal the red scarring beneath. The pattern on one arm almost made me look like a tiger, striped with angry red over paler skin.

Slowly I removed the rest of the bandages. There were a few of the larger wounds not quite fully healed yet, but I was mostly well, if very stiff. I wondered how long I'd been laid up.

I love a man with scars, Iomu purred within me.

Sometimes I wonder if you should have let another Lumani bond with me so you could have been a woman and enjoyed me in other ways.

I don't know if Dawn and Roo would have let me join you.

Ah, yeah, good point.

And I do love feeling your strength. It's amazing! Also, the way you can fight... none of my hosts before have been as deadly. It really turns me on.

You're a strange blood-thirsty little spirit, aren't you?

And you wouldn't have me any other way.

She was right, I wouldn't. I laughed a little.

Hearing what sounded like the noise of construction and carpentry outside, I rose and went to the window. Sure enough, the town was being rebuilt, and significant progress had been made, I'd been out for a while. But looking over the massive project and the many people working on it, something occurred to me almost instantly... there were too many people here. Even if all the non-combatants from the village of Dwa Brody — as well as others who'd come with us — had returned from hiding in the hills, it wouldn't account for this work force.

I heard my door open and turned to see Ceph entering. He still looked much weaker and somehow... reduced from the man he'd been before all of this, but there was a smile on his face and a certain lightness to his step.

"You're up, good," he said with a smile. "You can feed yourself today." He hefted the tray he carried, bringing it to the table next to my bed.

"I can, yes. How long was I out?" I asked, sitting to eat. It was simple fair, a cup of tepid tea, a hunk of bread, some milk and cheese, as well as some dried, sliced fruits and vegetables.

"More than a week."

I raised a brow and kept eating. From what I recalled, Ceph had had a sword through his gut, but seemed well enough now. "You healed quickly?"

"My avatar heals quickly and... Pan helped a little," Ceph said, and his smile turned a little sad. "It seems my... old ability... helps things heal a bit quicker than this new healer. She simply accelerates the body's natural healing by increasing its internal defenses. It causes fever, knocking people out, and from there they heal mostly on their own while resting."

Still, with how wounded I'd been, a week seemed like a short recovery time. I nodded to Ceph. I still had a lot of questions: "you said Pan helped you, so he survived. What of the others? Is the dragon lord dead?" I assumed so but needed to hear the words.

Ceph nodded. "Apparently it was quite the battle. Lyran is a bit upset he didn't strike the final blow. Pan did. All three of them were quite the sight when they returned. They'll all have scars. That wasn't an easy fight... for any of us."

Nothing about that day had been easy. "Agreed."

Ceph nodded.

Curious about the number of people outside, I asked: "It seems there are more people here than before. Did more come from Elista?"

Ceph smiled. "No. Well, a few more came, but some also returned." He gave a soft, breathy laugh. "Most of those you see outside are from the dragon lord's army. They... wanted to help. It seems most of them weren't true Thraians. Many were from a kingdom called Jural, if not from Basia itself. They'd been conscripted and forced to fight, but... once the Thraian generals were gone, they were happy to help. Many of them may remain here. It's a pleasant enough place. This village will be a town soon enough."

That was interesting and... good to hear. I was glad the war was over. "And Roo and Dawn?"

Ceph sighed. "You... no, I suppose you wouldn't know. Dawn was killed the day of the battle, or at least her body was incinerated when Swan died." I blinked at that, horrified and torn, my heart rending with loss and grief.

Yet Ceph went on as if he'd been describing the weather: "But Dawn's spirit was strong enough to remain after the body was destroyed, and it has merged with Roo. Dawn's spirit is in Roo's body now. She... they..." He quirked his face, then shrugged. "Roo is resting, as she has been for most of the last week. The merging was... *is* taxing on her. It doesn't surprise me that having two spirits, plus two Lumani within oneself takes some getting used to."

"Dawn is..." I was shocked, but glad to hear that she'd survived... sort of. My sorrow and grief remained but were well tempered. "Oh..." I was still just a little confused at exactly how this might have happened.

"Yeah. Roo has been asking how you are. I'll let her know you'll probably check in with her in a bit."

"I'd like that, thank you." Something occurred to me. "How is Pan handling this?" He'd been dedicated to Dawn alone and with Dawn's soul in Roo's body...?

"He took it hard. He still hasn't fully recovered. In his mind, Dawn is dead. He can still speak to her and is happy she's around, but he can't imagine being with another woman's body that happens to be inhabited by Dawn's spirit. It's complicated and he's... upset."

I nodded. I could imagine.

I ate in silence for a while. Ceph remained, keeping me company. It was good to have a friend near, even in silence.

"What's the plan now?" I asked. "We defeated the dragon lord and his armies. So...?"

Ceph laughed a little. It was good to hear that sound from him. Even though he wasn't fully himself, he seemed different, a bit more confident and spritely. "We've all be asking ourselves that. Dawn was the one who drove us forward so much we're all a little... uncertain without her. Lyran has achieved what he'd been trying to do for ages, well part of it at least, but he's nowhere near ready to take on all the rest of his brothers yet. So... We've just been waiting and helping the village rebuild and..." He shrugged.

"Ah."

Ceph rose. "I'll let Roo know you're coming. Finish up your meal, you're probably starved. When you're done, Roo is down the hall, last door, at the end. After that... the healer said you'd need to take it easy probably for a few more days, but knowing you, you probably won't. Talk to the twins if you're looking for something to do. They're heading up the rebuild."

I nodded, and Ceph left.

I finished my meal quickly. I wanted to see Roo again and find out more about Dawn and... yeah...

There were clothes laid out for me, but they weren't mine. I could tell just by looking they'd be too small. There were few men as large as I was. When I dressed, I ripped a few of the seams on the shirt and pants. Then, looking awkward and rag-tag, I left to see Roo.

I knocked on the door at the end of the hall. "It's Rhino."

"Come in," Roo called, voice soft and melodious.

I entered and there she was, reclining in a seat by the open double-doors leading out onto a balcony. The sun was streaming in upon her. She wore a gauzy robe and as she rose, with sun upon her, it was near to see-through, fully revealing her voluptuous form.

My cock hardened so quickly and thoroughly that — given how tight my pants had been — I burst the ties and fabric, launching my erection out to freedom as my pants fell to the floor.

Roo laughed, eyes going wide.

Then I laughed. It was just a bit ridiculous. She hurried to the door, closing it behind me, before whispering, "I'm glad you're happy to see me. I'm not sure if I'm up for that yet, but it's good to know you're still... as large and ready as ever."

"My pants were too tight," I said, then shrugged. "And you're too gorgeous. A bad combination."

"Or a good one."

"Or that, yes."

Pits! That was amazing! Iomu cheered within me. *THAT is why I love you, Rhino. Most women would love to have their man's cock ruin a pair of pants, all on its own, just because he looked at them. If I had one, my pussy would be drooling at that thought.*

I ignored Iomu and focused on Roo. She went to a wardrobe and pulled out a long piece of fabric, a wrap-skirt, bringing that to me. "For... when you leave," she said.

I nodded, taking the garment. She ushered me to the sitting area before the doors which led out to the balcony. She returned to the long reclining couch, and I took a sturdy, cushioned chair across from her. Since sex wasn't on the menu, I covered myself with the skirt she'd given me, laying it over my lap. That only made a rather awkward tent in front of me.

"That doesn't help much." She giggled.

I laughed. "Your fault, not mine."

"Oh, really? Can't control yourself at all?"

"Not around you, no."

She sighed out another soft giggle. "Thank you for that," she said softly looking away out the doors, into the distance. "I haven't laughed in some time."

"Because of... Dawn?" I asked.

Roo nodded. "It's been... difficult." A sigh. "Today is the first day I didn't swoon and get dizzy when I got up. Whatever we did... it seemed easy at the time, in the realm of spirit, but it took a toll on my body."

"But... she is well... inside you?"

Roo smiled softly. "Yes. Would you like to speak to her?"

"Can I?"

Roo nodded. "Yes. One moment." Roo stilled, closing her eyes. Then she... shifted. It was a subtle thing, hard to describe, but her body seemed to adjust into a pose which was more like Dawn would have taken, sitting a little straighter. When she opened her eyes, I blinked, stunned. The dark sable of Roo's eyes was gone, replaced with the shimmering gold of Dawn's. Everything else was Roo's body, but the eyes and the posture was... all Dawn.

"Hello, Rhino."

"Dawn?"

"Yes, it's me."

I shook my head. "I... know. I can see it. It's you, but it's not."

She nodded slowly. "I know." She stared out the window and... in that moment she looked a lot like Roo had a moment before; a little lost and uncertain. "Everything is different now. I'm alive, but my... my body is gone. I have no clue how I'm going to explain this to my mother."

Oh yes, the queen.

"Whatever you do, we'll all be there to support you," I said softly.

She smiled. "Yes, I know."

She rose and swayed a little. "Ohhhh," she breathed. "I'm still getting used to this body. It's... very different."

I rose, wrapping the cloth around me quickly. No

longer was I ragingly hard. I went to Dawn, helping her, and she leaned gently upon me as we walked out onto the balcony. There, she turned her head up to the sun, closing her eyes. "Thank you," she whispered. "It feels good to be... touched again." She sighed heavily. "I just want to feel the sun on my face and the wind in my hair for a moment longer, then I should return. It's taxing on Roo when we switch."

I took that moment to pull her close, holding her tight. "Then take this with you," I said and kissed her tenderly.

"Thank you," she whispered again. And I heard the emotion rising in her voice. I guessed that she hadn't felt an embrace, nor a kiss in far too many days. In this moment, it was all I could give her, and it was more than enough. "Good-bye," she said, and a moment later I felt the shift, even as I held her. The eyes that looked up at me a moment later were dark sable brown. Tears welled and, when she blinked next, a few moistened her cheeks.

"Oh..." Roo said softly. "Thank you, Dawn needed that." She reached up to wipe her eyes. "This is... going to take some getting used to."

I pulled her close. "And we'll do it together."

She nodded against my chest.

"I should rest," she said.

I lifted her easily and carried her to her bed, laying her down carefully. I remained, close, kneeling beside the bed and aching to be with her. I leaned down and kissed her softly. Her full lips responded instantly, opening, drawing me in. Her tongue beckoned mine. Soft and tentative quickly became hard and needful. Both of us had been resting for some time and it was clear, despite our wounds — inside and out — we both wished to have this now.

Her hands came to my face, one raking up through my hair to pull me closer while the other simply felt the contours of my cheek and traced over an ear.

I undid the tie of her robe and slid my hand under the sheer fabric to the smooth skin of her side, then up to the heavy swell of her large breast. She gasped as I massaged her fullness with growing intensity. My other hand came up to tangle in her hair, sliding behind her head to keep us close and deep.

She moaned softly into my mouth, hot breath bleeding out of our connection, before she tilted her head back and my hard kisses sought down over her chin and neck.

Her nipple was hard against my palm. I slid my hand over to push her robe open fully and pressed my lips to the rise of her other breast, the stubble on my chin scraping over her nipple. She gasped. But I quickly kissed it better plucking the rousing bud into my mouth, sucking hard upon the puckered areola. My hand slid to her hips, through her curls, then down. She opened her legs and my fingers dipped into her folds, seeking her core.

I dipped a finger within her and it came away wet. I used the lubrication to trace around her clitoris and her breath caught before she let out a shuddering: "Ohhhh. Yesssss."

A knock sounded from the door.

Roo groaned, shifting, whispering: "No."

I lifted back from her. "Should I stop?" I grinned. "Or should I ignore them and continue?"

Both her hands came up to grasp the sides of my face and force me back down for a desperate, deep kiss. I wasn't sure what this was, but I went with it.

Another knock.

She released me and sighed. "I should probably see who that is," Roo said. She added a whispered: "Sorry."

"You stay here, I'll get it." I rose as she wrapped her robe around her luscious form once again.

"Ohh... ah... Rhino?"

I nodded, realizing what she was seeing. The wrap around me was lifted and showing all my significant arousal.

I drew in a few long breaths, thinking of mucking out the barn on the farm back home. That quickly had me looking a bit more respectable, and I went to the door.

I didn't recognize the young woman on the other side.

"Oh!" She seemed surprised to see me. She looked up from my chest to my eyes, seeing my full height and size. "Oh!" she gasped, her eyes widening. I had that effect on people. I could be an imposing man. Yet, I smiled and held a relaxed posture, shoulders slumped and bent forward a little as I'd been practicing. The young woman's smile grew, and she blinked. "Sorry... ah, is Lady Roo here? A message has arrived for her?"

From behind me Roo asked: "A message? From whom?"

The young woman handed me a small container; the type used to hold messages attached to pigeons. "From my home, Osera. From Captain Myra," the woman said. Ah, so she was one of the Oseran refugees. I remembered the captain: a small, stocky woman, with a cocky grin and mop of dark hair. "I... I think it's urgent, though I didn't read it. But... before, when we Oserans used to keep pigeons and send messages, these red containers were always for the most vital messages."

I noticed the flaking red paint over the small container.

"Thank you," I said. "I'll take this to Lady Roo."

The young woman nodded and left.

I closed the door and went to sit on the bed beside Roo, who'd pulled herself up, propped on some pillows, to a sitting position.

I handed over the container; my large, thick fingers would have a hard time opening the tiny lid.

Roo deftly unsealed the container and drew out the small roll of paper within. She unrolled it and read aloud: "Osera has fallen. All the dragon lords came. They're heading east, to you."

My heart fell into my stomach. We'd had a hard enough time fighting one dragon lord. We'd have no chance against all nine of Aaghar's remaining brothers together.

"They must have heard about Aaghar," she whispered, her voice tense and quavering. "Now... they're coming for us."

CHAPTER 3

DAWN

WE ABANDONED DWA BRODY, HALF BUILT. WITH IT WENT any dreams of peace and freedom. War had found us once again, and this time... there was little hope of victory. It took several days, but Fin transported us all to Elista. A few stayed behind — Falcon and Swift among them — to act as scouts and let us know when the enemy got that far.

I knew all of this through Roo, knowing what she knew and able to sense the world second-hand through her. It wasn't the same as when I took control of her body, but I could still see and hear things, just... a bit removed from when it actually happened and through a sort of... filter... of how Roo experienced them.

Is this what it's like for you? I asked Amya and Leoa. I could speak to them both freely here in this strange place of spirit within Roo.

Yes, Amya said. *We experience everything you do, but through your personal experience of things.*

Oh.

And the rest of the time, I just floated within the beautiful panoply of Roo's spirit, filled with all the vibrant colors of life: bright yellows, blushing pinks, deep rose-reds, verdant greens and the pale blues of a summer's sky. It was a wonderous and peaceful place. And with me were Leoa, a ball of pink and blue, and Amya a smaller sphere of reds and oranges. I'd learned that, to the Lumani, I looked like them, a sphere of deep burning reds with flashes of golden orange and brilliant yellows and hot white, like a raging fire.

Every day, Roo and I grew stronger together. We practiced switching and extending how long I could be... out, so it wasn't as taxing on her when I took control.

And I'd need to take over in a moment.

Roo and I had been called before the queen, my mother. So far, we'd managed to avoid her, delaying the news of my death. For nearly five days we dodged our set times to meet with her. Even Midnight had only had a brief audience and not mentioned my death. We'd hoped to delay the inevitable, but the queen had finally insisted. I didn't know how I'd tell her, but I'd run out of time to think about it.

Are you ready? Roo asked. *We're here.* I sensed her stately, graceful walk and the presence of many others around us. We were in the throne room.

I am. It may be best to switch once you've come to a stop,

*we wouldn't want us to fall over ourselves in front of the
queen.*

I felt the smile, which twitched and tugged at her lips
at that thought. Roo resisted laughing outright.

She came to stand before the queen. I could see that
my father, Alvere of Vauphan wasn't on his throne, only
Queen Legs was in attendance today. Interesting.

Roo and I switched quickly, and I saw my mother's
head tilt slightly. I think she'd caught the strange change
of eye color which happened when I took control.

I came into full control of the body and Roo's senses,
and immediately calmed myself, which didn't take much.
I was incredibly impressed with the control Roo had over
her emotions, probably a side effect of her spirit-gift.

"Where is my daughter?" the queen asked, a hard
note in her voice. "I have demanded her presence, and
she has evaded me long enough."

I swallowed hard and took a long breath. I felt Roo
bolstering my courage, as well as the support of both
Amya and Leoa.

"Hello Mother, I am here, a passenger spirit within
this body. I'm afraid I've gone and gotten myself — or my
body at least — killed. Ah... sorry?"

I heard gasps and many murmurs from the assembled
Nobles and spectators.

For her part, my mother remained — mostly — stoic.
There was a tightening of the jaw, which only those who
knew her would have seen, and a hardening of those
russet-brown eyes.

"Dawn?" she said softly.

"Yes, it is me, Mother."

Very uncharacteristically, she rose from her throne and raced down the steps to embrace me with an intensity I'd never known from her. "I'm so sorry," she whispered.

So... this is what it took to get her to truly love me. I just had to die.

That's not fair and you know it, Roo said. *I can sense her emotions and she loved you greatly even before this news.*

I... know, but... still. This is the most emotion I think she's ever shown me.

She is the queen.

I know, but I'm a bit sick of that excuse.

Are you going to keep standing there, or hug her back?

Oh... right...

I drew her close, feeling strange in this much fuller and taller body. My mother seemed smaller now.

"It was my fault," I whispered back to her. "It was my choice. I... did Midnight tell you about Swan?"

"Yes. Though I'll kill Midnight for failing to mention this."

"We both thought it best if you heard it from me. I... I did what I had to, to defeat Swan. Her powers were great and the only way to defeat her was to kill her, and that... killed me in the process. But... I'm not truly dead. My spirit remains, and I was so closely linked to Roo that she was able to take me in, Bond like we do with Lumani."

I felt my mother's nod. "I'll need to have a long talk with Roo some time; thank her. Is that possible?"

"Yes, we share consciousness. You can tell who's in control by our eyes."

"Yes, I did notice that shift. It was quite strange."

She released me, but only a little, so we could look eye to eye instead of whispering over each other's shoulders. "I get the feeling there is far more to this story than can be told here, but... I did call for this audience, are you up for a bit of a summary of events?"

I smiled. "Of course, my queen."

Her lips tightened and I saw pain in her eyes.

I sighed and relented just a little. "Mother."

She smiled and tears welled before she blinked them away. "I... I love you, you know that, right?"

I cocked my head, wondering where that had come from. "I do, yes."

Liar, Roo teased.

Shut up.

"Good." She rose to her full height, stepping back to take a long look at me. She nodded to herself, then returned to her throne, sitting to become the stately monarch once again. "Report," she said.

I gave the highlights of our trip. And, as I did, I recalled that the entire purpose of Roo and I going initially had been to prevent war with Thraan. We'd utterly failed in that. We were now bringing war to Elista's very doorstep, probably far quicker than it would have come, and certainly a far greater force than it might have been. But... we also brought allies: Oserans, Basians, Thraian deserters, Northerners, and Njor-vasoturi.

Even as a recap, it was a long tale, and I could feel a bit of strain starting on Roo's body. This was the longest I'd ever been in control.

"Thank you, my daughter and Lady Roo," the queen said. "You may retire for now, but expect a summons to a private audience for a full report within two days. We will need all the information we can get, to weather what is to come." She nodded, and I was dismissed.

I quickly gave Roo back control, and we left the audience chamber, returning to our room to rest.

Our room, where four loving men waited for us. Falcon and Swift were still away scouting in the west, but the others were staying with us. Pan was... distant. The other three made us comfortable, tended to our every need: fetching food and drink, massaging our aching muscles.

I need to talk to Pan... alone-ish, some time, I said to Roo.
I know.

There hadn't been the time since we'd returned, and before that, he'd mostly been avoiding me... us.

But after a meal and a short rest, we were feeling better and stronger. Our bond truly was growing. "Please, if you all wouldn't mind leaving for a moment?" Roo asked. "Dawn would like to speak to Pan alone."

The other three nodded and left.

Roo and I switched again, it was getting easier, a

smoother process. It helped this time that we were propped up in bed, resting.

Pan came to sit on the bed, close, but he couldn't look at me.

I reached out and tugged on his arm, bringing his hand out and holding it tenderly.

"It's not your touch," he said softly. "It... if I'm not looking, I can almost feel you there. The way you hold me is the same, but... the hand is too big, too soft."

He was right. My hands had been calloused from hours of daily practice with weapons. Roo, however, did not like fighting and had learned only the basics of what she needed to defend herself.

I squeezed his hand. "But it is me."

He flinched. "The words are yours, but the voice isn't." Very slowly he turned his head to look at me, and there was pain in his amethyst eyes. "I can see you, but it's like you're behind a veil. Every touch is marred, every word is skewed, only your eyes are the same." He swallowed hard. His words stung, piercing the already heavy ache in my soul, and I bled anguish and fear. "I love you, Dawn, and I always will. I... I hope you know that, but I can't be with you while you're like this. It's hard to even look at you."

"Roo is beautiful," I whispered.

"She is," he conceded softly. "But she's not you. She's like... a sister to me. And if I were to be with you now, I..." He shuddered. "It just wouldn't be right... at all." His features tightened and a tear leaked from an eye down over a pale cheek. "What if she bore our child?" he whispered.

"Would that be so bad?" I asked. Certainly, Roo's more womanly body would have an easier time in childbirth than my smaller and slimmer physique.

"It wouldn't be *our* child. It would be hers. Even if it had some spark of your spirit, it..." He turned away, shaking his head.

His pain is... deep, as deep as yours and just as jagged and cutting, Roo whispered within us.

I didn't really need her to tell me that, I could see it well enough, but I knew she felt both of our sorrows deeply, and that couldn't be easy for her.

"I... want to be with you, doesn't that matter?" I asked softly.

"It does, very much. I want to be with you too, but..." He shook his head, more tears upon his cheeks. "Those are not your lips, even if it is you behind them. I... I hope you understand," he said, voice growing choked and soft.

I did. It didn't stop my desperate ache to be with him; to hold him and be held by him. Yet he wouldn't even go that far.

He drew in a long breath, sniffing back tears. "I love you Dawn, and I will do anything you ask of me. I have Ceph's powers and perhaps... there is a way to... remake your body? I don't know, but I will try. I'll do anything for you, for us, but I can't be with you, so please don't ask."

I wouldn't. I couldn't help my own tears as I whispered: "I love you too, my heart, my love, my life, my amazing Pangolin. We'll find a way to be together again."

He nodded.

And already I was thinking I might know how. I squeezed his hand. "Remember... that time when you were with me in spirit? What if I could make that happen again?

He turned to me then, hope blazing in his eyes. "I would love that," he said softly.

Do you think you can? Roo asked. She was well aware of the... oddity of that one circumstance, when the guys had brought me back from being lost within my own mind and soul.

For him, for all of us, yes, I'll make it happen. I think... I think it may just be the only true way for all of us to be together.

"As would I," I said. "I'll make it happen. It may take some time to figure things out, but I'm far more connected within my spirit now than I was then, I do not think it will be too hard. We'll be together again soon, my love."

He nodded. "I look forward to it, my heart," he said, his gaze intent upon my eyes, focusing there as he smiled. "I love you, Dawn." He swallowed hard. "I'm sorry."

I squeezed his hand again. "I love you too. Thank you for this. I know this wasn't easy for you. Thank you."

He nodded. Closing his eyes, he lifted my hand to his lips and kissed it softly. Then he quickly released it and rose. "I'll tell the others they can return," he said, wiping his eyes.

"Thank you," I said. I relinquished Roo's body back to her. This time, we hardly felt drained. Though the tight twist of my emotions still didn't make me feel... good about any of this.

We'll find a way, Roo said.

Yes, we will, I said, determined, sure.

She laughed inwardly. *That is the Dawn I know, always so sure and strong.*

I knew I hadn't been feeling so strong recently, but slowly... I was starting to feel like myself again. I sent Roo a sense of certainty. Then I looked inward, recalling that time when I'd been with Lyran, Pan, and Swift within my spirit. I needed to remember all the details so I could remake that event.

I'll help any way I can, I remember it well, Amya said. I felt his reassurance and hope.

Thank you, Amya.

I would do it. I would be with Pan again and at the same time I'd be helping Roo experience something amazing.

CHAPTER 4

FALCON

I FLEW NEXT TO MY BROTHER AS WE SLICED THROUGH THE
air, winging our way to Elista. It had been nearly three
weeks since we'd seen any sign of the dragon lords. They
were moving slowly. As much as the lords themselves
could move with devastating speed on dragon-back, their
armies on land could not, and it seemed they meant to
gather as large an army as they could to bring against us.
We'd found their camp, already massive, larger than
Aaghar's army had been. And every day, more and more
men arrived from the west. It was almost an unending
line of soldiers pouring into the camp. Other Elistans
with bird forms were staying behind to get a final count,
but Swift and I were desperate to return to Roo and
Dawn. So, we'd been sent back to report our findings thus
far. Our message would not be one of hope. Already the
dragon lord's camp numbered close to three hundred

thousand men. Even if all of Elista and Vauphan gathered every man from their armies, they'd not have more than a hundred thousand. We were already outnumbered three to one, and the enemy army was still growing. That alone may not have been too discouraging, yet when you added in the nine dragons and the powerful lords that went with them...

But there was cause for hope: one of those dragon lords might be on our side, if his promise remained. The second eldest son, Ensar had helped us escape from Thraan. We all hoped he'd keep his word and turn on his brothers. But even with Ensar and Lyran on our side, that was two dragon lords against eight, still not promising numbers.

Falcon? The voice within my head sounded like Dawn's. I flinched and nearly fell from the sky. I caught myself. From Swift's reaction, it seemed Dawn had reached out to both of us at once. Interesting.

Dawn? How are you doing this? I replied as if I was talking to Eluei, my Lumani.

I have learned a lot about spirit in the last few weeks. I am... stronger now than I was before. I'll have a surprise waiting for you when you return. I sense you are already on your way? Yes?

Yes. I cannot wait to get back to you and Roo. Somehow the thought of being with them together, both in the same body, was intoxicating. I could pleasure two women at once; a thrilling thought.

That would be interesting indeed, Roo chimed in, responding to my thoughts.

Did you hear that?

It was more of a feeling than actual words, but I got the picture well enough. I'm looking forward to it too.

How are you able to be here as well? I asked.

Dawn and I both have learned a lot. I was the one who found you, sensing your emotions. Dawn was the one who made the connection with you, and together we are able to speak to you.

Fascinating!

Indeed. Dawn was back. *Roo and I eagerly await your return, our twins. Fly to us with all haste.*

I... there is dire news, I said, my spirits falling. *The dragon lords are gathering men. We'll have to report to the queen. Things are not looking good.*

We know, Roo said. *We don't know the specifics, but I've been reaching out farther and farther with my spirit-gift. Dawn and I combined are... quite strong. We've sensed the mass of gathering men, if not the exact number. Do what you must when you arrive, but hurry to us.*

I will. We will.

Actually... I had an idea. *If we tell you everything we know, you'll be able to tell the queen, that will save us some time.*

Yes, it would. Tell us everything.

We relayed what we knew. We didn't know exactly, but our guess was that the dragon lords were waiting for an army of at least five-hundred thousand. We estimated, given how many men arrived daily, this would take another month or so.

I will tell my mother, Dawn said. *So, when you get here, hurry to us. We have a gift for you, a very special gift.*

I can't wait!

I felt the presence of the two women I loved fade from me. I cried out as only Falcons can and looked over at swift. There was excitement in his eyes. We communicated with far more than words as well, our spirit-gift an intimate bond between us.

What do you think their surprise is? I asked Swift.

I have no clue, he responded.

Any thoughts? I asked Eluei.

I am at a loss as well, but I love surprises. I am certain it shall be wonderous indeed.

As am I.

Both excited and eager to return to the arms of our lovers, Swift and I put on even more speed to hurry home to them. We'd originally planned to be at the capital by mid-morning the next day, flying and resting in turns. Spurred on now, we went without rest, as fast as we could and saw the lights of the city by sometime in the middle of the night.

Here... Dawn said. And with the word I felt a pull. I followed it, coming to a window to alight on the sill. Roo waited within. Swift landed next to me and together we hopped into the room transforming as we did.

Everyone was here, Roo — and by proxy, Dawn — and the other four guys. They'd been waiting for us. Everyone seemed eager. Roo wore only the gauzy shift she'd worn a lot since combining with Dawn. The guys were each naked except for a special loincloth.

"Join us," Roo said, coming to us, handing Swift and I both the same garment. "Put these on."

I raised a brow in question.

Roo smiled. "We'll explain as you get changed."

I began stripping off my clothes and Swift followed suit.

"Dawn and I have found a way to be with you all. All of you at once, and—" she addressed Pan specifically. "—with whichever of us you wish to be with, or even both at once." She smiled enigmatically. "We have been strengthening our gifts, and we've discovered how to join with you all in spirit, in the same way some of you once did with Dawn." Suddenly Roo shifted, her eyes turning gold, and Dawn was speaking. It happened almost seamlessly. "And the best part is, you can be however you wish to be in the realm of spirit. You can be alone with one of us, or together with all of us, or with some and not others. Each of you will experience something different and unique, while Roo and I will be with each of you. We've found a way to split ourselves within the realm of spirit. And you'll be able to do it too. You can live out any fantasy you like, for in this realm anything is possible." She sighed. "There is but one downside... your physical bodies." She looked around at us. "They will experience what your spirit experiences and trust me, it will be... quite intense."

Lyran laughed, a knowing sound.

Swift had told me of his time with Dawn in her spirit and how transcendent it had been. I looked forward to it. But he'd also told me of the rather extreme mess the four of them had made physically. Suddenly I understood the need for these special loincloths.

"That is why you have the wraps you do, so we won't have to wash down this entire room afterward." By then, Swift and I were changed and ready. The two of us sat, and when Dawn joined us, that completed the rough circle on the floor. Several cushions had been placed for our comfort.

"Ready? Just lie back and... enjoy!" Dawn — in Roo's body — demonstrated, reclining on the pillows.

I was more than ready, despite the long journey here. Suddenly my fatigue was gone and all I wanted was to enjoy my time with Roo and Dawn.

I lay back, closed my eyes, and felt... a pull. I let it happen and a moment later I was in a world of swirling warm colors: hot, deep reds, rich plum purples, and brilliant golds. I was just a bit shocked at the beauty of it.

Welcome to your own spirit, Eluei said in her silken voice. And her ball of energy appeared nearby, a mass of dark purples and deep blues.

This... is my spirit? No wonder it felt so... right!

Yes, young one.

Come to me... the voice seemed like some distant whisper, and with it I felt another pull.

Your lover calls to you, Eluei said softly. *I must admit, I am very curious about what is to come, I have never experienced such a thing... at least not through a True-Bonded. We Lumani have ways of merging our spirit forms, but that is... very different.*

I am quite curious as well, I said. Then I let myself be pulled by Dawn. Though I didn't truly go anywhere. I remained within my spirit, but I felt like I... merged with another... no... two others. One was all fire, and I knew this was Dawn. The other was filled with the serenity of nature and love: Roo. They enveloped me, surrounded me, and I felt at home within their spiritual embrace.

This is a place without form, but if it helps, you can give yourself form, Dawn said, and she appeared floating before me, coalescing from the fiery spirit around me. She looked as she had in life... except that the gold of her eyes was now a smoldering fire. And beside her, Roo appeared with eyes which swirled with colors of a perfect summer's day.

The two of them came to me and I felt my arousal keenly. I had not yet taken form, but when I concentrated on a vision of myself... I think I focused a bit too much on the wrong thing.

Oh! The two women gasped as one, as my erection stretched up to match my own height before my face.

Dawn laughed. Perhaps we should have mentioned that in this place, you can alter your self-image. She shimmered and suddenly her breasts were fuller and heavier, legs longer and slimmer.

I looked at Roo. She shrugged. *I have no wish to alter anything of myself.*

No indeed.

I concentrated on my massive cock and shrunk it down to a more reasonable size.

And in truth, Dawn said, *size doesn't really matter here. We are already within each other as deep as any will ever get. You will be a perfect fit for us and we for you. Since these are not true physical forms, they are... malleable. They merely serve as a way for us to enjoy what is to come in a way we are more familiar with, but in truth we do not need them.* She waved a hand and suddenly my skin was on fire, tingling with an extremely enjoyable, full-body, near-orgasmic, pleasure. *Now, you try.*

I didn't really know what I was doing, but I tried what she had done, moving my ephemeral hand, while at the same time imagining the utmost of pleasure enfolding her.

Ohhhh! Yes! She moaned softly as every hair on her body stood on end and she shuddered. *Yes! You learn quickly.* Her breasts seemed to swell again, the pale pink of her areolae darkening as her nipples came to stand stiff. Her body flushed, that amazing blush upon her perfect pale skin. Her legs parted just a little. I... felt her heat, her desire, her need.

She and Roo came to me, their not-physical bodies pressing close. But I still felt... everything keenly, perhaps even more acutely than I might have physically. These bodies seemed to exude their desires. Roo whispered, *how would you like us? Would you want others here?*

Yes, I did. I didn't even have to say it, they knew. And Swift was there with us. So was Ceph. I hadn't realized how much I liked the man's willingness to experiment and play. In this place, Ceph was strong and tall once more, not the shrunken version of himself from the real world. The five of us pressed close together, bonding, merging as we sent our essences out into each other; a slow, sensual dance of building bliss.

I was everywhere among them. With a press and push I was slipping inside the wet embrace of Roo's folds, but somehow she was also stroking me with both hands, while teasing my tip with her tongue and lips. Dawn moaned as my fingers deftly pressed and played on her clit, but at the same time I was thrusting in long slow strokes, deep within her, while she took swift in her mouth. And Ceph was inside me, but also somehow thrusting through me into Roo. My lips kissed and sucked over the pale swells of Dawn's breasts, while other hands massaged and pressed upon Roo's fuller bosom. It was the most intense and arousing moment I'd ever experienced; intimate and powerful. I felt like I was alone with both women, yet also together with the others and all our spirits were dedicated toward a single, mutual pleasure.

Dawn moaned and shuddered through a small orgasm, but her passion only built from there.

Yessss. She drew out the word, then begged: *harder.*

Now I was suddenly in both of her openings, driving deep with forceful thrusts, as her legs wrapped around me, hard, pulling me closer.

Roo gasped and pulled me close to grind down upon my cock, pressing deep within her, as she came in a trembling rush of emotions. *I love you,* she whispered. *More... more!* She embraced me, pressing her softness to me, close and warm and inviting. Ceph was there with us, pressing close behind her, with patient thrusts which seemed to drive her mad. But then suddenly Ceph and I were switched, and I was the one behind her, slow and steady, feeling the tight press of her rear opening up for my swollen erection.

This is amazing, Eluei breathed. *I can't get enough!*

And neither could I. My erection throbbed, aching to release, but I wanted to bring even more pleasure to my lovers before I did.

Dawn's voice came as a whisper behind my ear. *You can come all you want in this place and never grow weak. Don't hold back!*

Oh Spirits, truly?

So, I didn't wait. Pressing deep inside Dawn and Roo... and even Ceph... I unleashed my hot torrent. And within me Ceph released as well. And somehow, I knew Swift and Ceph were also filling our lovers with their floods at the same time. A wave of ecstasy blossomed from all of us, but mostly from Roo. She seemed to explode in bliss, sending waves of it cascading through each of us, carrying us higher and farther into a transcendent rapture. More than just my cock, but my entire being seemed to be deep inside my lovers, exploding with every bit of essence I could give them. My heart, no my body, no this entire place pounded with ringing intensity as we merged and released and came together to merge once more, in an unending wave of perfect euphoria.

And that... was only the beginning.

CHAPTER 5

PAN

Yessss. Dawn drew out the word, then begged: *harder!*

It was just her and I, floating in peaceful bliss within our merged spirit. My colors: midnight black, dark amethyst, and dusky raspberry red had merged with her fiery, hot hues just as our imagined bodies had merged in a passionate embrace.

This is... Eona had no words. She was still a young Lumani, having had only one host before me and such an extreme and intense experience as this was one she had probably never considered possible. I felt her shudder with bliss and purr with delight.

Dawn was in the midst of a series of small orgasms, building and building in intensity as I pleasured her in every way. I was deep in her folds, but also thrusting from behind. She stroked my cock with her hands and filled her mouth with it. My hands were everywhere upon her, needing to feel all of her, now that we were finally alone together, as she'd promised.

This is perfect! I whispered, a hot breath on her ear. Even though I knew — distantly — that she was being with all the others at the same time, I didn't care. She'd made sure I had my moment with her and that was all that mattered. *I want... to give you everything. I'd give you my life, if it would bring you back!*

I know, my love, and I need you too. Her hot whisper of need drove my desire to new heights. *Of all the men here, you are the one we need the most. Your power is treasured and invaluable. I need you to connect with me, even deeper than you are, to share it with me, with everyone. Then, perhaps I can be remade one day!* She pulled me close, legs wrapping around me. Her various openings contracted around me, pulsing and milking my erection, desperately urging me to release. *Give me everything,* she whispered. *You can come all you want in this place and never grow weak. Don't hold back!* Her own bliss shuddered through her, trembling with such a powerful need, yet to be released.

I surged: harder, more desperate, deeper. I gathered everything that I was: my gift, my Bond with Eona, Ceph's borrowed gift, even my Fey abilities with metal and earth. I was a massive force of energy and spirit and when I cried out with my release, I poured everything I had into Dawn. She gasped and cried out, swelling with the puissant gift I was giving her. Her spirit form blossomed and bloomed with radiant power and eminence. Then she exploded in her own release. A powerful wave of spirit washed over me, and I was exalted to the highest point of pleasure, a pinnacle of bliss so acute and forceful that I seemed to swell and grow myself. And I simply pushed all that divine rapture... back into Dawn. She too rose in exaltation. Back and forth we surged within each other, a true and abiding exchange of spirit and love.

And I knew then, even if she never regained her body, this would be enough. Joining her in spirit would always be enough... more than enough. Just this one moment would be enough to last me for ten lifetimes of love for the one woman I had always adored. I had given her everything, nothing held back, and she had given me all of herself in return.

I love you Dawn, so much, forever! I cried out. *My heart, my life, my spirit are yours!*

And I am yours, Pan: my heart, my life, my spirit. I love you with every fiber of my being.

I wept tears of joy at her words, wonderfully and truly fulfilled in that moment.

Such... love, such passion and spirit. I... I... love you too, Pan, and you as well Dawn! Eona was bubbling over with affection and appreciation. She redoubled my passion, and I threw myself back into loving Dawn.

And Dawn had been right, I didn't grow weak. My passion and stimulation didn't fade or flag. I remained strong and continued to drive her mad with bliss, giving her all my essence again... and again... and again... and again.

CHAPTER 6

RHINO

In this place of spirit, I wasn't too big. No body modifications were needed for me to thrust hard and relentless into the women I loved.

Dawn gasped. *Yessss.* She drew out the word, then begged: *harder.* As if I wasn't already slamming impossibly hard into her... all of her. I'd rarely been able to fit inside the rear opening of Dawn or Roo, large as I was, but now... I was full and forceful inside that tight and throbbing canal.

But more than that, I was equally as deep within Roo, and... everyone else was here with me. It was an orgy unlike anything we had experienced before. Even that day of bliss in the glade of the Maraslad Forest had been... limited by the physical world. But in this place of spirit, within my own realm of rich, dark, earthy browns, rust reds, and deep, dark greens, anything was possible. I felt everyone else's colors merging with my hues. And we all focused our love on the fiery force of Dawn and the serene peace of Roo.

Yes, harder, use all your strength! Iomu screamed within me, delighting in the pure force and dominance I could assert in this place, without fear of harming anyone.

I love you, Roo whispered. *More... more!* The intensity of need in her voice drove me mad, and I was so desperate to make the most of this improbable moment that I found myself swelling and releasing uncontrollably within her... within both of them. I was worried I had come to soon, but Dawn chuckled and whispered: *You can come all you want in this place and never grow weak. Don't hold back!*

So, I didn't.

She was right. Despite the torrent of my flowing release, I remained ready and hard, continuing my devastating thrust as Roo and Dawn were driven higher and higher, climbing the mountain of their bliss. And then... Roo unleashed a torrential wave of pure and powerful pleasure surging through me. I felt like she was coming within me, and I felt the warmth of it spread from my stomach up into my chest and through my body. I pulled my two lovers close, somehow thrusting into both of them, as they wrapped their legs around me, driven mad with need. And though I should have been too tall, too big to reach their lips for a kiss, I wasn't. I pressed my lips to both of theirs as one, pressing their bodies close to my hard form.

We need all of you, all of your strength! Roo gasped. *Give everything to us, and we'll return it to you a hundred-fold!*

Pits yes, we will! Iomu called back.

Roo laughed, a sound of pure joy. *It's a pleasure to meet you Iomu. I'm glad you relish in Rhino's strength. So do I,* Roo purred that last part, then moaned loudly at my unrelenting assault of pleasure.

Don't encourage her, I said. *I'm pretty sure Iomu's fantasy is for me to thrust you into pieces, destroying you with ecstasy. She's a vicious and blood-thirsty Lumani.*

It wouldn't be the worst way to go, Dawn said, shivering and shuddering with a release upon my cock. *Go ahead, give it a try.*

Are you sure? I asked, uncertain.

Yes, Dawn and Roo said as one. Dawn continued: *destroy us with your release, Rhino. We'll remake ourselves after. Anything is possible here!*

Spirits!

Yes, do it! Iomu was driven mad with violent lust.

I roared, redoubling my ferocious thrusts within them, I hadn't stopped coming, but now I surged forth with everything I was and everything I had. I possessed strength beyond human capacity and through my merged spirit with these two amazing women I gave them my gift. They'd said I could alter myself in this place, so when my next powerful orgasm hit, I imagined my cock swelling to impossible proportions before exploding with my heat and passion into my lovers.

Yes! they cried out as one. *Yes!* Their voices rose with

the intensity of their combined bliss. And they seemed to swell also, filled with my heat... before they exploded, shattering with the highest extremity of rapture. Roo drove her emotions into me, and I couldn't help but combust with them. My body-image became a million shimmering shards of condensed bliss while my mind and spirit overloaded for just a moment with the impossibility of what I was feeling.

Then... all the pieces of myself, Dawn, and Roo coalesced and reformed. Remade, we gasped and writhed and moaned, shivering with the aftershocks of that heavenly experience.

And though I had poured everything I had into them, I didn't grow weak, I didn't fade.

Again! Iomu laughed.

Yes... please! Dawn gasped. Roo nodded, wordless.

And so continued the purest moment of unsurpassed joy in my entire life... and it didn't end. It flowed and ebbed and resurged and washed over me as I gave myself wholly and completely to the women I loved.

CHAPTER 7

LYRAN

I LOVED WITH THE FORCE OF A DRAGON. EOPHON'S SPIRIT was joined to mine, and in this place of spirit, I was a dragon indeed, ultimate in strength and vigor. With us were Rhino and the twins, as I knew they'd wish to be with both women together, and that is exactly what we had, in this strange place. Dawn and Roo were separate but also one, just as I was one, but also many, loving both women. And I knew, even though I hadn't invited them to my fantasy, that Ceph and Pan were loving their respective partners as well, somehow, somewhere.

My cock had never felt so full and robust, nor had it ever felt so perfectly accepted within a woman as it did within both of my lovers now. Usually, I was too long for either of them, but here I filled them perfectly and each long thrust was a powerful demonstration of my love for them.

I held Roo close, driving her to greater heights of bliss.

Her hot breath on my neck whispered: *I love you. More... more!*

So, I gave her more, her and Dawn both. I embraced them fully, in front and behind, surrounding then in my power and love as I filled their spirit with my raging desire, pulsing in time with theirs, ready to explode in a geyser of unrelenting bliss within all of us. And I waited, on the brink of my release, holding it as I gave them my all, ensuring they were far gone into pleasure before I finished.

Dawn's voice came as a whisper behind my ear. *You can come all you want in this place and never grow weak. Don't hold back!*

INDEED? I HAD BEEN IN THIS PLACE BEFORE WITH DAWN, had experienced the odd joining which happened here, but this was new to me. Yet still, I wished to prolong the bliss I gave for as long as possible. So, I split my essence into four, each as powerful as I was, but engulfing both women, in front, behind, wrapped around. In this way, I could unleash myself in waves. One part of me — taking Roo from behind — cried out as I let slip my control and with a wild series of thrusts burst forth within her.

Yes! Roo cried out. *We need all of you, all of your strength!* Roo gasped. *Give everything to us and we'll return it to you a hundred-fold!*

While still in the midst of a mind-blowing orgasm in one part of Roo, I did the same in Dawn. Then again in Roo, in front. Then again in Dawn. I let out a four-fold draconic roar as I fully unleashed my spirit and all that I was into them. And my cry was matched by their unified shouts of bliss. And a moment later, as promised, I was hit with a wave of power and pleasure so strong I lost all sense. All I knew was that I would happily give everything I had, everything I was, to these women. Reverberating waves of bliss bounced between us in an eternity of ecstasy until I was simply a conduit of power and joy into them... and they into me.

I roared forth again, feeling stronger than I ever had before.

At the same time... somewhere, out in the real world... a true dragon roared with me.

CHAPTER 8

CEPH

IN THIS PLACE — OF SHIMMERING TEAL, VIBRANT MAGENTA, and bright lime green — I was whole. I was myself once again, powerful and proud, unbent and unbroken. I and all the others except for Pan drove ourselves to pleasure Roo, to bring her to such heights of passion as she had never known before. We worked in concert, many essences combining with a single goal. I felt them, their intensity and need, their drive and desire to give everything to this wonderful woman... and to Dawn as well.

I could feel Dawn. She wasn't here in this place with me, but she was such an integral part of Roo now, that some essence of her was here. She was a being of spirit and through Roo had made all of this possible. She united us and also managed to keep each of us within our own fantasy; our own realm of spirit. And for that I thanked her and wished to give to her everything I had as well... through Roo.

And everyone can feel my ultimate supremacy! Ulio roared.

Shut up Ulio, I said with a sigh. *This isn't about you... or even me. This is about giving to others, shut up and pay attention, you might learn a thing or two.* I tuned them out after that and hoped they would learn from my dedication to others.

I took my time with Roo. Yes, my desire raged and overflowed to be with her, inside her, but I also felt such a deep and abiding love for her that I wanted this time to be special. I didn't know when I'd be able to be with her like this — as strong as I was now — again.

Ever since burning myself out healing Lyran, I had been impotent, unable to bring myself to arousal. I was a broken man in many ways, and yet Roo still loved me. She had, for some time, slept with me, holding me close while I had trembled and whimpered in the night. I had been truly pathetic, but she'd never stopped loving me. And for that, I loved her all the more and wanted to show her exactly how much. So, I kissed her gently, my lips upon hers, plucking and pulling, playing with their soft fullness. I spent an eternity focused on her lips, hearing her soft moans and delighted giggles. At the same time, I'd use the unique properties of this place to arouse every inch of her skin. My hands were everywhere upon her, soft and caressing, tracing lines of tingling bliss upon her. Every inch of her had become excited gooseflesh, puckered and aroused. She seemed to vibrate with bliss as she rode the waves of several soft and sensuous orgasms, even before I had entered her. She was so overcome with the extremity of this tender bliss that she wept tears of pure joy, shivering and full-body blushing as I took my time with her.

Hmmm, yes, Roo breathed as I kissed my way down from her lips to the heavy swells of her breasts. I traced my tongue around the stiff peak of a nipple before plucking the large areola fully into my mouth with heavy suction. I could feel the beat of her heart pounding through the sensitive flesh between my lips as she moaned and shivered beneath me. I flicked my tongue over the nipple again and she gasped. Releasing that breast, I paid similar treatment to the other before kissing lower still.

Her legs wrapped around my neck as I traced her slick folds with my tongue. She moaned louder, unabashed as her hips pressed up, seeking deeper, firmer attention. I glued my mouth over her clit and sucked hard again, lapping with my tongue, while exploring her opening with three fingers, as she was so incredibly aroused. She shuddered and released, flooding over my fingers. I drew her wetness out, moistening her swollen and flushed folds in preparation for my cock.

Splitting myself, I continued to caress all of her sensitive flesh — plying tender kisses upon her lips, breathing hot, soft words of adoration into her ears, stroking her hair and kneading the sumptuous fullness of her breasts — as I finally pressed my raging erection upon her. I felt powerful and virile as my cock pressed into her, filling her completely.

Then I heard Dawn's words echoing to me: *You can come all you want in this place and never grow weak. Don't hold back!*

But even then, I hadn't wished to seek that pinnacle of desire just yet. I took my time and sought to truly touch Roo's soul with my affections and attentions.

Roo breathed the words: *I need all of you, all of your strength! Give everything to me and I'll return it to you a hundred-fold!*

Only then did I begin to drive toward my final bliss. I knew I was behind the others. I began to feel the reverberations from them and Roo, echoes of powerful orgasmic essence moving back and forth, empowering both sides.

Ceph, you are a wonder, Roo whispered, her words just for me, seeping like a warm balm into my soul. *I love you and I can feel how much you love me. You have always shown it to me and here you have taken such pains to dedicate yourself to me.* Her words rose, trembling and breathless — even though there was no breath in this place — as she soared upon the wings of euphoria, driven higher and higher by the power of this place and this moment and all the love she was receiving. *And not only me. You gave everything of yourself to Lyran to save him, even though it meant losing so much of yourself. So, this... this is for you...*

And such a wave of power and bliss hit me that I was consumed by it. My release came, powerful and strong, filling her, yet I felt it only distantly. I was overcome with an incredible amount of strength and healing, a divine remaking energy.

I knew then why Roo had asked for strength from the others: it was for me.

I wept in joy as I felt myself being rebuilt, my soul and spirit remade, even... my body slowly healing from wounds I thought permanent. This was my gift. Pan must have given it to Dawn who had remade it and, with the power from the others, they had pushed it into me. I felt it... my spirit-gift being remade, re-instilled inside me. This was the power Dawn had mastered in her battle with Swan, the ability to take and remake a person's spirit-gift.

Thank you, I breathed, barely able to contemplate what had happened.

But I knew now... I was whole. My gift had been restored as had my body.

Roo was too overcome with the rapture of the moment to respond, but I felt her love and her joy at my rebirth.

Revitalized, I dove back into that place of spiritual bliss and sought to bring Roo to even greater heights of passion.

CHAPTER 9

ROO

THANK YOU, C<small>EPH SAID</small>.

Dawn and I had used the power and energy collected from all our guys to instill his gift, given by Pan. And with it, we had healed his body at the same time. I felt the extremity of his joy and elation, a feeling which words could never fully express, and it warmed my heart.

That was amazing, and powerful and I can't believe we did it! Leoa breathed within me, surprised and elated.

It worked! Dawn was overjoyed, both at the success of our secret plan, but also... the sheer amount of over-whelming pleasure and power all our men were pumping into us. It was unlike anything I had ever felt before, we each had five men thrusting and driving their powerful releases into us.

Dawn was giddy with it: *How does it feel to have five cocks in your pussy at once?* she asked, her own voice quavering with her recuring, intense orgasms.

It's unlike anything I've ever felt before, Leoa commented. *It's amazing!*

It's so much more than just that. I gasped. *It's the fullness of their feelings, the power of their spirits. No physical sex could ever compare to this!*

I know, right? I felt Dawn's own joy at my surprised elation.

The men were everywhere around me, not just five of them, but multiples of each. They were filling my spirit with the fullness of their desire, the intensity of their love and devotion. I had never felt so... loved. I had also never felt such powerful spirit-shaking orgasms before. The pureness of their passion was instilled directly into me, and the distillation of that desire meant a truly mind-blowing, world-shattering release multiplied by five! And when I used my spirit-gift to push what they were making me feel back out to them, it amplified the entire experience to a dizzying level.

And it was clear, they didn't want to stop. With strength in this place not limited by physical fatigue and not hindered by the loss of potency after a man released, no one wanted to leave this joyous moment; most especially myself and Dawn. In here, we were goddesses of spiritual and sexual power. When we returned to the living world, we'd still be two souls trapped in one body. Even with all the power we were receiving from our guys, we couldn't fix that. Though, we did have hope that with Ceph's power restored, perhaps he and Pan might be able to work some miracle.

So... we all lingered here for what felt like a joyous eternity.

But eventually the needs of our bodies called us back to the real world. We'd spent all of a night and most of a morning within our spirits and we were all famished and exhausted. It seemed extensive spiritual activity could fatigue the body as well.

When I slipped back into the limited confines of my body, I shivered. I was still tingling with the residual power of so very many orgasms.

Thank you SO much Dawn, Leoa seemed on the verge of joyful tears, if she'd had eyes to shed them. *I am fairly certain in all my lives to come I will never experience anything like that ever again. It was incredible.* And since Lumani lived for new experiences, that was saying a lot.

All of us sought the basins of now-cold water Dawn and I'd had put around the room beforehand. We spent a bit of time cleaning ourselves. Our bodies had reacted quite extensively to that spiritual bliss. Then we ate and drank and rested, relaxing for most of the rest of the day.

An invitation came for me to attend a dinner with the queen. I could bring two guests, so I chose Rhino and Lyran. The twins were doubly fatigued from their long flight the previous day while Ceph and Pan already had their heads together trying to figure out a way to create a body for Dawn and somehow get her spirit into it.

It was good to see Ceph filled with such vigor: straight and strong and vibrant with life once more.

Dawn and I rested before dinner, sleeping soundly for a couple hours before the guys roused us and the three of us dressed for the occasion. I wore a stunning gold dress, which hugged my figure and set off the dark honey of my skin. My hair was left long and unbound, flowing around me. Lyran and Rhino looked like warlord-kings with bits of ceremonial armor on their large frames, dressed in dark blue for Lyran and deep mahogany red for Rhino. They marched on either side of me, and I felt like a princess or queen myself as I made my way through the halls of the palace. Dawn would take over once we got there, but for now she let me enjoy this powerful moment.

When I'd left home less than a year ago — though it felt like a lifetime had passed — I would never have imagined two powerful men, my lovers, escorting me to dinner with the queen. And with the power and peace I felt after that amazing spiritual love-making session I was floating like a cloud when I glided into the queen's private dining room.

The large table already had many important figures around it. Lady Skyfire was here, along with Lady Dove and Lady Blackclaw, strong allies and friends of the queen. In addition, were several of the queen's retinue. Lord Ant was there, a big man but not as large as Rhino. Lord Silence was quiet and watchful. Lady Sparrow presented the image of serenity. Lady Midnight was... observant and wary, even here.

I had to smile when everyone in the room —
including the queen herself — looked up at me in awe,
staring. Since I had very keen hearing, I heard the queen's
barely audible comment: "Spirits, is she glowing? She's
gorgeous!"

Mom! Ewww! Dawn shuddered inside me, and I had
to keep from ruining my serene composure with a guffaw
of a laugh. Instead, I nodded to everyone and took my
seat. Lyran and Rhino sat on either side of me. "Thank
you for having me," I said with a nod to the queen. "I'm
assuming you'd like to speak with your daughter?"

"I would, yes, but I'd also like to speak to *you*, Lady
Roo."

Oh? Dawn was curious.

"Oh?" I asked softly.

"From your report, you were the one who went to the
heart of the empire and met the various princes, the
dragon lords who are now threatening us. What can you
tell me about them?"

I nodded slowly, resisting the urge to say: *they're a
bunch of loathsome, spoiled, men-children.*

I mean... that description isn't inaccurate, Leoa said.

*I figure she's looking for a slightly more diplomatic and
informative answer.*

Leoa gave the impression of a shrug. *Up to you.*

"My report had all of the basics, their names and hier-
archy, so I'm assuming you're looking for further
insights?"

The queen nodded.

I drew in a long breath. "They are contentious, to say the least; constantly vying for power and dominance. Ati Kaan is essentially the emperor. He keeps his father in power, but the man is almost completely mad, mindless. The First Prince also keeps his brothers in line with his dragon-gift, the ability to read minds. He knows what they're planning and has woven a web of plans around himself to account for their schemes."

"And Ensar, the second son? Do you believe he will truly turn against his brothers?" Queen Legs asked.

I shrugged. "I honestly don't know, but he was certainly... different from the rest. I sensed genuine benevolence within him, a desire to help. His wife has been a good influence on him. And I can't deny that he helped me, and those with me, out of a nasty situation. I can't imagine why he would do that if he wasn't sincere."

"Perhaps to set up a deception later on?" the queen postulated. "If they let you go, then Ensar might be able to pretend to defect and get into our good graces before betraying us at a critical moment."

"That... is possible." I hadn't thought of that.

You like to think the best of people. My mom and I are a bit warier. Dawn was also clearly skeptical.

True.

"He would have to truly prove himself worthy to become an ally," I said. "If he does more damage to his brothers in defecting than he might within our own ranks, that might go a long way to making him a bit more trustworthy."

The queen nodded. "True, we shall have to see what he does and when. What of the others?"

She knew of their various abilities, but I reviewed my assessment of them. "Ati Kaan is always in control but doesn't seem to make a big deal about it, at least not to his brothers. He prefers to let them fight amongst themselves than go against him. Hakan, the third prince, thrives on a sense of power. Since the first and second don't flaunt their power, he does. He'll take any chance he can to make others feel week or powerless. Burak, is quiet and unassuming. As such, I didn't get a lot from him. He could be dangerous, but if so, I don't know how. Mesik is a nasty piece of work, thriving on humiliating others. He knows he can't match his brothers for true power, so he just makes himself feel powerful by making his minions — and sometimes his younger brothers — do horrid things. Nurgul, Bayar, and Okan weren't there, so I didn't get anything from them." That left Demir. I hadn't included all of what had transpired with Demir in my report to the queen. Certainly not the gory details of our encounters, nor the fact that I'd castrated him. "Demir is a troll. A short, fat man who thrives on inflicting pain on others, every type of pain. That's what makes him feel powerful." *And cutting off his cock made me feel powerful.*

You are a devil, aren't you? There was grim satisfaction in Dawn's tone.

It depends how far someone pushes me. Demir... I shuddered. Dawn's spirit and mine were open to each other, but our minds were not. Yet still, I'd told her everything that had happened, we had no secrets between us.

I'd have done the same thing, she said softly.

I took a little comfort in that.

"Will they fight amongst each other?" the queen asked.

My assessment was: "Yes, but only in secret, off the battlefield. I think they are... fairly unified in their desire to crush us. We killed their brother and all of them will wish to avenge him... in their own way. They'll work together to make sure it happens, or so I believe."

The queen nodded. "Thank you. Anything else about the Thraians which might be of use?"

"They are proud and confident. They know their armies vastly outnumber ours. Their confidence comes from a justified place, but it is their weakness. If we are able to rout them, able to defeat them, their confidence will start to waiver. Then, perhaps the brothers might turn on each other."

"Good to know, thank you." The queen smiled, but there was a strained quality to it. I felt her awkwardness. I guessed she was trying to figure out how to ask to speak with Dawn without being disrespectful to me. I helped her out.

"If that is all, I will summon Dawn."

"Yes, please."

Your turn, good luck, I said as a gave control over to Dawn.

I'll need it.

Oh, shut it! Your mother is lovely.

Still, I felt Dawn's own awkwardness as she took control. Now I was but a passenger, hearing and seeing, but no more. I could still feel emotions, though, and watched the table with all my senses.

"Hello, Mother," Dawn said softly.

The queen's demeanor changed. Everyone here were family or close friends, and I felt her odd combination of ease — that she could speak freely, not as the queen — and unease, probably at what she was about to ask.

"Your report was... a bit light on details," she said slowly. "I'd like to know — if you're willing to tell me — how...?"

"How I died?" Dawn had a way of saying the hard things in a blunt manner.

"Yes."

I felt Dawn's awkward acceptance of that horrible situation. "I... I don't think anyone could have defeated Swan on their own. When you fought Merlin, you had your friends to help you. They got hurt because of it, but do you think you would have won without them?"

"No." The queen shook her head, saddened and sincere. "But... then, why did you go against her alone?"

I knew the answer to this one.

"Because the previous time I'd fought her, she'd used my friends against me. I... couldn't risk their lives, couldn't risk them being a distraction. I had to fight her alone so I knew... nothing would happen to anyone but me."

I felt the queen's turmoil at this, and the related confused sorrow from the others at the table. They had been willing to fight and die for Legs, for the nation, and some of them had lasting wounds from those fights with Merlin. But... Dawn was right.

The queen's voice was soft. "I may have a *hero*-gift, but... I think you're more a hero than I ever was, my daughter. You spared your friends from pain and potentially death, by sacrificing yourself." She sighed heavily. "I understand now."

Silence hung over the table.

After a long moment, the queen drew in a long breath. "But... you are able to take a person's spirit-gift? That is... a dangerous and terrifying power."

"Indeed," Dawn said softly. I felt how scared she was to even possess it. "It is not something I wish to ever do again."

"Do you... regret your actions?" the queen asked.

Dawn replied quickly. "No, not for a moment. I'd do it again in a heartbeat."

"She's her mother's daughter in that," Skyfire said in a wry tone. "Stubborn and sure of herself."

"Look who's talking," the queen said just as dryly.

Skyfire shrugged with a grin.

But the mood fell a moment later when the queen said. "Swan... was out for vengeance against me, but you're the one who died. I..."

I felt her emotions: guilt and remorse, an intense longing to have saved her daughter from this tribulation.

She doesn't know what to do about that, I told Dawn. *She feels responsible.*

As she should.

Go easy on her.

Why?

Because... she does love you and it's killing her that you've died... for her, for the kingdom.

I felt Dawn's heavy sigh. "Better me than you," Dawn said softly. "You're the queen. I couldn't let her get to you. I did what I had to... just like any other loyal citizen would have done. It is what we must do. Also... you're my mother, and... I love you and... I'd do anything for you..." Dawn's voice cracked then, grief and sadness welling, tears in her eyes.

I felt her pain. She would truly do anything to get her mother to notice her, to show love for her, to recognize her.

I felt the queen's anguish at this. She had no words. She knew she couldn't deny Dawn's logic. It was the queen's duty to protect her citizens, and the people's duty to protect their queen. Instead, she rose quickly and hurried around the table. A moment later we were being embraced and held tightly to the queen's chest. She whispered: "I love you, Dawn. I'm so sorry I was never there. I love you so much, I'm not worthy of a daughter like you."

No, you're not, Dawn said within us. But her spite was failing, her heart opening.

Really Dawn? I prompted.

Well, she wasn't... not before... but, maybe now...

That's a start.

And I felt the last remnants of the walls around Dawn's heart finally break and crumble. She choked out the words: "I love you too, Mom," as she sobbed upon her mother's chest.

CHAPTER 10

CEPH

I FELT BETTER THAN I HAD EVEN BEFORE THE INCIDENT IN the Maraslad forest. I felt amazing. My body was strong and hale, I could take a deep breath without coughing and run for miles before tiring. My spirit-gift had miraculously been returned to me by Dawn and Roo, and I was eternally grateful to them, and the other men in our little group, for making that possible. I was myself again, and ready to take on the world, which it turned out, I'd need to do.

I'd just been made a general in the Royal army. With everything that had happened since I'd left Elista, I'd forgotten that I was actually a member of the Royal House. I had just assumed I'd join with Roo in her house, but... That hadn't officially happened yet. There was too much to do and the nation was sorely in need of generals who'd seen significant action to lead the army of Elista and their allies... and what an army it was.

Every possible Vauphani soldier had been called to Elista. They'd left their eastern border completely unguarded, having ceded large swaths of land to Fiore, their eastern neighbor. It would be a small price to pay if they stopped the Thraians now, on someone else's soil. They alone had forty-thousand light infantry, fifteen-thousand heavy infantry and twelve-thousand heavy cavalry. Next to them, the Elistan army was a bit less impressive: roughly fifty-thousand men, mostly light infantry with a bit of cavalry and heavy infantry here and there as special units among the Noble House Armies, which were now combined into one.

We also had eight-thousand Fey, small but mighty. They had come down in droves from the north, ready to protect these lands and stop this invasion before it came to their home.

Then, there were the forces we had gathered from the west. The largest group was the roughly twenty thousand men who'd defected from Aaghar's army. There was also a small force of Oserans, led by Captain Myra. These were not the civilians who'd come with Roo, but those who'd survived the onslaught of the dragon lords and the fall of the island nation, only about four hundred or so. Commander Lucjan and Lord General Makar — Myra's cousin and father — had not survived that final assault. Finally, there were the Njorvasoturi. More of the Njorvasoturi had found their way south, in response to the summons going out across the north. They were a fearsome fighting force of roughly two-thousand men and women with over two hundred Karhukora mounts.

All told, our army was roughly a-hundred-fifty-thousand man and women. A significant force indeed. Yet the word from our scouts in the west had the empire's army at over one-and-a-half million and still growing. We estimated we'd be facing an army of two million or more, outnumbered roughly twenty to one. But considering we'd been outnumbered two hundred to one at Dwa Brody, I thought we were doing quite well. Most of the other generals did not share my cheery outlook.

The real wild cards in the coming fight would be the dragons. They had nine to our one. Even if Ensar switched sides, eight to two didn't seem like great odds. But Eophon was different, far stronger than they had been, thanks to Pan's use of my gift, in conjunction with his ability with metals. Even so... it didn't seem like we'd be able to hold off their dragons. And a dragon was worth... ten thousand men or more.

But we still had time, so we made the most of it, by preparing the various fields of battle for the coming invasion.

I was overseeing the preparation of what we anticipated to be the first battlefield. In the west of Elista there was a town called Cragmount. Grizzly House had their fortress — Stonehold — nearby. The craggy hills of the area made for lots of interesting places to stage ambushes or funnel the enemy into kill zones. We'd make our first stand here. If that failed, another field of battle was being prepared near the capital. We'd make our last stand there. We wouldn't have time to prepare any other places and we assumed that if we lost twice, our armies wouldn't have any strength left in them. Our options were defeat the Thraians or die trying. It was sad to think that one of the "best" outcomes would be if both armies destroyed each other, with millions of lives lost, but having saved our nation and those beyond to the east. Hopefully, it wouldn't come to that... or anything worse.

As I helped my men in their work, digging trenches. I felt Ulio grumble. *We're a general now, we don't have to do menial work.*

I mostly ignored my pesky Lumani, but in this, I had to correct him. *You're right, Ulio, we don't have to do this work, but every hand is needed right now, and my men will be motivated to work harder if they see their own general getting dirty. I won't have any man in my command grumbling and complaining about the work they're doing and how their officers are just sitting there, doing nothing. I expect them to work just as hard as I do, and I won't give them any excuse not to. And... that includes you. No grumbling allowed. Either I'll survive this, in which case this work will have been useful, or I won't survive this, and you can annoy your next True-Bonded.*

Ulio sighed and shut up after that.

The day waned, and I called my troops up from digging earthworks and pitfalls to rest. A night shift took over, we worked around the clock, but the men I commanded were done for now.

"Returning to the capital?" General Fin asked as I entered the command tent.

I nodded. "Yes, please."

He smiled, looking exhausted. He'd been ferrying people around for weeks now. There was a small group of us here, who'd return to the capital for the evening. We joined hands and Fin snapped us instantly to a courtyard in the capital. I swayed, still not used to that mode of transportation, before steadying myself.

Then... I hurried to see Roo.

The six of us who loved Dawn and Roo had been separated from each other and our loves as the preparations for war had developed. The Twins were captains now, under Lyran. Elista had tentatively accepted the once-dragon lord, but only if he had 'minders' and such were the twins to him. Pan was the liaison to the Fey. He'd been given a rank of Lieutenant. Rhino was the least practiced of all of us and had been given a rank of Sergeant and worked alongside Captain Myra with the Oserans, helping to train them in hit and fade tactics, making her forces into a guerrilla troop. We were all busy but had arranged a schedule to return and visit Roo and Dawn.

As it was, Roo wasn't being let out of the palace grounds. She would be an asset in any fight to come, so the queen had restricted her movements. She was too valuable to be out in the field, so the justification went. Roo was well with this, but Dawn hated it. One of the few things the two spirits in one body disagreed upon.

I burst into her room, and she smiled from where she sat next to a large washbasin. She been expecting me.

"As I suspected, you're filthy. Let me bathe you." She wore a simple wrap around her torso, nothing more. She looked stunning. Her long, auburn hair had been combed out, falling in waves to mid-back, and her dark-honey skin glistened in the lamp-light flickering around the room. Her large, sable eyes beckoned to me, hooded and heated.

I smiled, closing the door behind me and quickly disrobing, discarding my armor and clothes, both of which were heavily stained with sweat and dirt.

"Sit." She directed me to a stool within the washbasin. She sat on a similar stool next to the basin with her feet in the waters of the large low tub. I sat and she leaned forward, drawing me to her for a soft, long, sensuous kiss. Our lips met and pressed, played and plucked before opening to deeper pleasures and the soft moans of hot breath which followed. By the end, my cock was rock hard and ready, but she smiled at my arousal and picked up a sponge. "Only when you're clean," she whispered.

"My thoughts are anything but clean," I whispered in return.

"Thoughts don't count. If they did... I'd need to bathe too."

I blinked at those words and smiled. Roo wasn't usually one to be overtly 'dirty' in her lovemaking. Perhaps Dawn had been affecting her a little.

She washed me slowly, taking care to scrub the dirt

away. She took special care with my face, and once it was clean, she kissed it softly, all over. I reached up between her legs, wanting to give her something in return, but she swatted my hand away. "Your hand's not clean, yet."

"My lips are," I said suggestively.

She gave a breathy laugh. "Yes, but if you started kissing me there, I don't think we'd finish this bath."

"True."

She washed my hair, running her fingers through it to comb out the dirt, rinsing with a basin of warm water, which cascaded down over me. I reveled in the wet warmth... hoping I'd soon be enveloped in another sort of wet warmth.

She moved down my body slowly, torso first, then arms and hands. She took her time, drawing out this sensuous time and the building tension which went with it. She wanted us to be fully on fire when we merged. And she knew that once my hands were clean, I'd reach for her. And I did. Though I didn't go for her legs like before; instead, I turned toward her and carefully unwrapped the cloth from around her. Her breath hitched as it fell away. She was already aroused, I could see that clearly, her nipples taut, large areolae flushed and swollen. I caressed her, keeping my hands above her waist as she continued my bath. I stroked her arms and hair, cupped her cheeks, slid my hands down her sides, then brought them up over her stomach to feel the full weight of her breasts in my palms. This happened to coincide with her — very attentive —

cleansing of my erection. And for a long moment we lost ourselves in stroking the sensitive flesh of the other.

Finally, she spoke, breath coming hard. "I should finish your legs..."

"Yes," I said softly. "Your legs."

Her washing became a bit more vigorous over my thighs and calves, then finally my feet. I, in turn, was concentrating on her legs as well, my hands hard upon the ample flesh, making sure I'd caressed her all over before I dove inward to her slippery folds, which opened at my touch. She gasped, more swiftly scrubbing my feet as I stroked her deeply and brought her arousal to a near-peak.

"They're clean enough," she gasped and then moved into the basin with me, straddling me. She lowered herself — with a long shuddering sigh of bliss — upon my cock. That heady wet warmth I'd sought earlier enveloped me as I pressed deep within her. She moaned as she pressed her body close to mine, her lips next to my ear. "No more hands" she whispered. "I want to feel just your wonderful cock for a moment." Then she kissed my ear before drawing back. I let my hands fall away as she drew her own hands up into her hair and above her head, swaying in a sensual dance upon my lap, the tips of her breasts brushing against me, which seemed to send thrills through her. She was so amazingly sexy and volup-tuous. I felt my own arousal keenly, my peak aching, even as I used my gift to keep me at that pinnacle without release, my erection twitching with desperate need inside her.

She let out a shuddering breath as she ground down upon me, hard and needful. She'd been close to a release before and with her hard rocking upon my shaft, she quickly came to a full-body, muscle-tensing, pussy-clenching release.

She let out a long moaning sigh as she brought her hands back to my head and urged it down to the fullness of her breasts. "Hands are fair game again," she gasped as she savored her ecstasy. I brought my hands back to caress her further, stroking her legs and sides and feeling the fullness of her round, heavy buttocks. My lips played upon her bosom, covering that soft expanse with kisses or plucking and sucking on the tender but stiff nubs of her nipples.

"You've always been so tender and careful and loving," she whispered. "I love you, Ceph. I'm so glad you've returned to me."

"As am I." And I was truly and deeply grateful. I was forever indebted to Dawn and Roo and Pan, who together had given me back... everything that I was. And I would, for the rest of my life, give everything for them.

Roo began rocking upon my erection once more.

"More?" I asked, hiding my own desperate need to release, wanting to give her everything first.

"Of course," she whispered.

"Am I clean enough?" I asked.

She giggled. "I don't know about your feet. You'll have to keep them on the floor."

A challenge? Accepted.

I stood slowly. Roo wrapped her legs around my waist and her arms around my neck, keeping herself in place, as I moved to the bed.

I sat her on the side of the bed, and she released her arms to lie back upon the soft mattress. She squirmed upon the blankets, shifting her hips to massage my erection within her. Her eyes were filled with mischievous fire.

I wouldn't come so easily. I unwrapped her legs from around me an brought them up so her ankles rested on my shoulders. I kissed her feet, leaning forward a little to thrust down into her. I grabbed her thighs and pressed them together, closing her canal around me. It had flushed and opened with her previous release, but I wanted her to be tight and feel every inch of me as I thrusted deep, slowly and gently.

She gasped and squirmed at my relaxed and tender pace. "Your cock feels so big and ready to explode, but still, you take your time with me. Such... a tease!"

"A tease? If you wish," I said and moved a hand lower over her belly, slipping a thumb down between the pressed legs to the rigid bud of her clitoris, leisurely but forcefully rubbing and pressing.

"Oh, spirits!" she gasped, and her hips began a faster movement. She wanted me to match, but I didn't. I kept myself slow as I drove her crazy. But her aggressive thrusting paid off for her as she tensed once again, gasping and moaning through another long orgasm. Her opening clamped down upon me, drawing me deeper, milking my cock in hopes of my release. My body screamed at me to give her what she wanted, my erection painfully tight with incredible pressure from my held passion. And still, I kept my slow pace, which only seemed to drive her crazy, prolonging her pleasure, drawing it out until she let her legs fall down limp to either side of me.

"Spirits, you're so damned patient, just... take me!" she said heated.

I leaned down to kiss her softly, first upon the lips, then over her breasts as I spoke slowly. "You want me to take control?"

"Yes."

"To make you mine, and only mine."

"Well for tonight at least."

I gave a breathy laugh. "Of course." Then a thought occurred to me. It wasn't my usual way of doing things, but... "Do you want me to command you, to possess you, to roughly take my pleasure on you?"

"Spirits, yes! Stop talking and do it!"

"Shall I become... your master?" I tested the waters with this. I'd been talking to Rhino and Swift about their times with Dawn and taking control in such a way. In truth I had no real desire to be in control, but perhaps Roo liked that fantasy?

"Master?" She tested the word. I could see the hesitancy behind her eyes for a moment, but then... some-thing in her shifted. "Yes... master." Her dark eyes filled with need, wanted this. "Take me, master. Make me yours. I want only to please you, master."

As much as I hadn't thought I'd like this fantasy, the way she looked at me now — those dark eyes so full of desire to please — made my aching cock swell even more.

"Oh, yes master, I can... feel you master."

So... what would I do with this? I smiled, then pulled out of her suddenly. She gasped. I forcefully rolled her over as I grabbed a vial of oil from the bedside table. I dribbled the thick liquid down between her butt-cheeks and began massaging her other opening. "Up, on your knees!" I commanded, and she obliged, pulling knees up under her, but keeping her head down, wiggling her large, round buttocks. With my height, she was now at the perfect level. I pushed her legs together again and forced myself back into her folds, while my fingers played in her other opening. No longer was I patient and slow. I thrusted with force, watching her buttocks shake with every hit. And she gasped and cried out with the force of my affections.

I slid my one hand down her back then around to her front. "Get up," I growled. I helped to lift her as she came upright, leaning back against me. I still had two fingers playing in her puckered rear opening, but the other roamed over her front, from caressing her soft breasts to violently stroking her clitoris.

She came, hard, crying out as I drove relentlessly

inside her. But I wasn't done. I kept up my ministrations, prolonging her orgasmic throes, urging them higher, to another, more intense orgasm. Her body went into fits, shaking violently as she let out wordless screams.

And between her vicious cries, she tried to speak: "Yes! ... Master! ... Please, master... I want... I w— oh! Yes! I want to... make you come, Master!" When her fits eased a little, she laid her head back on my shoulder. "Please," she begged again, eyes pleading.

I smiled. "If you want to make me come, tell me how much you want it. Tell me all your filthy thoughts." Roo was usually restrained in how she spoke during sex, but I wanted her to talk dirty now.

She gasped, her voice lowering to a breathy whisper incredibly laden with lust and desire. "Please master, I want to feel the hot rush of your come in my aching pussy. I need to feel your cock pulse inside me. Fill me, master. Impregnate me. Come master, come in my pussy!" She licked her lips, mouth open.

I felt my cock swell, ready and full, but held my release for just a moment longer. First, I kissed her, claiming her open, panting mouth. Then, I pushed her down to the bed once again, knowing I'd be able to get deeper inside her for my final thrusts. Her hands grasped the blankets, bunching them into her fists as she quivered and bucked. I removed my fingers from her other opening, it was ready, open and waiting. Good.

Grabbing her hips, I slammed myself into her, driving hard for my release and sending her into fits once again.

"Yes, I will come, but not in your pussy," I growled, then I pulled out and pushed hard into her other opening, the oiled entrance accepting me deeply.

Her cries escalated an octave, and I felt a rush of wetness upon my balls as her pussy flooded. I pushed deep into her ass and cried out as I let myself finally release. As my cock pulsed over and over, filling her, I used my gift to spread tingling bliss through her loins, shooting out to all parts of her body. She came again, screaming, and bucking hard. Her opening gushed with her own hot release, the moisture dribbling down both our legs.

We stayed locked like that for some time before she squirmed. I was only just finishing, so potent had I been, and I withdrew slowly.

She flopped over to her side.

"Spirits!" she breathed. "I... I wasn't expecting that switch at the end. Spirits! Wow." Her voice was hoarse and rough. She shivered and her body broke out in gooseflesh, still achingly sensitive it seemed.

Then she giggled. "Did you like my naughty servant girl?" she asked playfully. "That felt so... strange."

More than I had thought I would. "Yes, surprisingly. But next time, I want to be the naughty servant and have you command me."

"Done!" she said with another giggle. She relaxed a little more, spreading out on the bed. "That was amazing, thank you. Dawn and I both thank you... she felt all of that. Sorry, I can't help but share."

I understood.

"Why don't you join me" she asked patting the bed beside her.

"My feet are unclean, remember?"

She giggled. "Oh, right. Sorry. Well, go clean them and join me, I want to feel you wrapped around me tonight, all night."

"I'm not going to get much sleep, am I?" I said returning to the basin to scrub at my feet.

"Nope, you can sleep in the short periods while your cock is recovering, other than that... I'm going to be a demanding vixen."

I had asked for that. I smiled.

I'd pay for this tomorrow, but that wouldn't stop me from enjoying it fully tonight.

My feet finally clean, I scrambled up onto the bed with her, enfolding her in my arms, pressing close.

She pushed me away. "You'll kiss me when and where I tell you to, boy!"

I smiled, feeling my cock twitch and start to harden. "Yes, Mistress."

CHAPTER 11

DAWN

I WAS FURIOUS THAT I HAD TO REMAIN HERE AT THE CAPITAL while the battle was fought out there. My guys were putting their lives on the line, but I was being treated like a porcelain doll for fear the tiniest touch might shatter me. I raged, while Roo soothed me.

The day of the battle had finally come. Months had passed and the army of Thraan was indeed over two-million strong. But we'd had lots of time to prepare, and the battlefield was ours to control... or so I'd been told. I'd never been there.

I want to be there; to help! I shouted within Roo.

I know. I want to help too, and I might be able to, even from here.

Well, then, let's do that. At least it's something.

I'll probably need your help. Leoa and Amya, we'll need you too.

I'll give you anything you need, I said.

And we're here to help however we can, Amya added for himself and Leoa.

What's the plan? I asked.

I might be able to reach that far with my emotion sense and hinder the enemy or bolster our troops, but... I don't know, it's a long way. Your power with spirit to connect to others, would probably help.

Yeah, I can do that.

Already I had feelers out. Roo and I were inexorably close with our six guys and even when they were far away, we could feel them. I could sense their spirit, and Roo would know what they were feeling.

So, I started with that.

I knew roughly where our guys would be on the battlefields from their various descriptions of their assignments. Lyran would be on Eophon high over the battle, waiting for his brothers to strike on dragon-back so he could harry them. Rhino was close to the front, his shock troops, the experienced veterans from Osera, were hidden in tunnels below the battlefield to pop up and hinder the enemy advance. Swift and Falcon were with a line of archers in a secure position, firing down on the advancing armies. Ceph's division of men would be some of the first to be engaged, but they were still behind the others, waiting to march into battle once the enemy had been softened up. Some of the Fey were dispersed into the army to aid and provide versatility to units, but Pan was with the main force of Fey, not far from Swift and

Falcon, close enough to the battle to use their odd powers to affect the enemy.

I reached out to Rhino first, since he was the furthest forward among our guys. I felt him, and through Roo, I felt his nervous excitement. He hadn't engaged the enemy yet and the anticipation of battle was both a weight upon him and a drive within him. Roo sent him — and those with him — courage and hope. Through my spirit-link I sensed his smile. He knew where that had come from.

Then I linked to Lyran, and Roo did the same. He too laughed and grinned, growing confident.

Swift and Falcon I could link to as one, since they were linked by their own spirits. We bolstered them, and the men with them, sending them a bit of courage and bravery.

Pan and Ceph were a bit harder to reach, as one of our connections with them wasn't as strong, but we managed send them a bit of encouragement as well.

Then... I sought out across the battlefield.

And I felt the horde of the enemy...

Oh, Sweet Spirits! I gasped and my shock flung my spirit sense back to me. Roo's body shuddered and we would have fallen, if we hadn't already been sitting, propped up with pillows on our bed.

So many! I gasped.

I had known, theoretically that the enemy was over two million strong, but to feel it, to sense that massive group of people, was something else.

I know, but we don't have to affect all of them at once, Roo whispered, soothing. *Try to find just the front, those going into battle first. If we can weaken them, that will help our troops.*

Listen to Roo, she is wise, Amya added.

I knew that already.

Yes, you're right. I would have drawn in a long breath, if I'd had a body. As it was, Roo was already staid and serene and didn't need it. She relaxed back into the pillows as I reached back out to the battle.

It was harder this time. I'd used up a lot of energy with that first pass. But Amya and Leoa lent us strength, and I was able to reach the front lines of the enemy.

Fighting had begun. The enemy were exerting themselves — though I couldn't tell what they were doing exactly — and men were already dying, their spirits winking out. I connected with as many as I could, perhaps as many as a hundred thousand? I couldn't quite fathom the number and counting was impossible.

Your turn, I said to Roo, strained while holding the connection.

I felt the pull from Roo, the harsh capturing of their determination and drive and yanking it out of them, leaving them empty and questioning.

We couldn't really see what happened then, but I sensed things, which suggested a couple of outcomes. First, the enemy stopped their advance, or at least moved far slower. That gave our archers more time to pick them off. Second, another wave of enemy troops charging in behind the first suddenly hit a wall of confused and disoriented men. Some were trampled, some accidentally killed on the weapons of their allies, but mostly it just caused more chaos and slowed the enemy advance.

I withdrew, exhausted from the effort of what we'd done, and I could tell Roo was as well.

We've done what we can, she said softly.

We'll do more, after we've rested.

Yes, she whispered and already she was lying back against those pillows heavily.

Anything more... at least for now... would be up to our guys. I wished them luck as I sank into a restless respite with Roo.

Just... stay alive, I whispered and felt Roo's agreement.

CHAPTER 12

RHINO

I SIGHED, FEELING READY FOR WHAT WAS TO COME. I should have been terrified as I heard line after line of the enemy marching above me, but Dawn and Roo had soothed my fears. The nearest exit to this tunnel — like so many others we'd dug through these rocky lands — slanted up with stairs to a heavy wooden board. The board had been inset down into the ground with earth on top of it to match everything around it. No one would know there was a hole there. And in just a moment, I'd be charging up out of that hole, throwing that board aside to surprise the enemy and charge with my small force right into their midst. I had been feeling a combination of terror and excitement, but then I'd felt... a sense of calm filter through me, and with it a surge of hope and courage.

It could only be Roo. Somehow, probably with Dawn's help, she'd reached across hundreds of miles to me and given me exactly what I'd needed before this fight. And with it, a precious reminder of what I was fighting for. I had a family to return to, women I loved and men who were like brothers.

Knowing the Oserans with me had lost so many of their loved ones — one of the reasons why they fought — I whispered to Sergeant Bolek, the Oseran behind me: "For our families."

He nodded then passed on the whispered exhortation, which passed back down the line.

Almost time, Iomu said within me. Her usual blood-lust was tempered today. She knew I wouldn't be able to stay and fight once we were among the enemy. That wasn't the purpose here. *Fare well, you big lug,* she said to me, then began a countdown starting at seventeen. She'd been keeping track of the timing needed to coordinate our attack with others about to do the same thing.

And when she hit zero, I surged up the earthen stairs, pushing on the board and throwing it up high over me as I drove into the middle of an enemy line, my sword in one hand, slashing wildly to cut down three men in close formation. With two more quick strikes to the surprised foe, I made a spot large enough for a few more of those behind me to gain the surface and that's how we attacked, slowly spreading out from our hole. The fighting was fierce once the enemy got wind of what we were doing, but by then we were already retreating. The point of our raid wasn't to stay and fight, but to disrupt the enemy.

Make them think every inch of ground was trapped or filled with foes.

I guarded our retreat and was grimly satisfied to see that none of our soldiers were left on the field. Though that didn't mean none had died or been wounded, only that we'd taken them with us.

I was the last down the hole and I pulled out the support at the end of the tunnel, which would cause a bit of a cave in behind us. They'd be able to dig through it eventually, but we'd be long gone by then.

That was exhilarating! Iomu purred, happy with the blood we'd shed so far.

You'll get many more chances to slaughter the enemy today, just wait.

I will.

We ran, carrying our dead and wounded, down the long, dark tunnel, then out into the light. Other Oseran forces, and several other elite troops from other tunnels, were funneling back to the spot behind our archers where medics and healers waited.

Captain Myra, looking grim and filthy — I probably looked the same — found me. "What's your count?" I did a quick survey of the fifty men and women who'd gone with me. "Eleven out of commission for now, five of those may never rise again."

She grunted. "You fared better than I. I lost a full third of my force and only half are still battle-ready." Her jaw was tight. She was chastising herself.

"It says nothing about you or your people," I said

softly. "Only that the fighting where you were was fiercer."

She nodded. "Still." A heavy sigh. "I'll check with the others. The regroup location is the same. We'll divide the forces among the surviving commanders and be ready for the next fight. It's going to be a long day."

"Indeed."

She marched away.

"Come on men!" I shouted. The remaining thirty-nine of my soldiers rose and followed me. Today was far from over for us. Sergeant Bolek got them moving.

Many tunnels had been dug under the battlefield by Elistans with Lumani who were natural burrowers, or even just by the hard work of a hundred thousand men and women. Our shock troops would keep popping up among the enemy and harrying them for the rest of the day and the next day and the next, until we ran out of tunnels.

I left my men for a moment to run up to a command station. Ceph was there. His entire force had yet to engage. But from here I could see the battle.

"Spirits," I whispered. From within the tiny part of the battle I'd been in, it was impossible to see the whole of the enemy. It was far easier that way, knowing all I had to do was pop up, kill, and retreat. But up here, I could see the massive expanse of their forces. "I can't even tell where we hit them."

Ceph pointed. "See the little eddies within the flow of their march? It looks like a bit of a circle? That's where you hit them. They're stuck there, as others move around them."

I did see it now, like churning wheels of men amidst the massive wave.

"How are the archers doing?" I asked.

"Well, I think," Ceph said. "I don't know how many they've taken out, because the enemy just keeps moving forward, but... something odd happened to the Thraian lines a while back, causing confusion. The archers laid nearly all the men to waste."

"Roo," I said softly.

"Did you feel her too?" he asked.

I nodded. "And I'm guessing she affected the enemy as well."

"Impressive if it was her, that was a massive swath of men who just... stopped."

"Estimates on how long we'll last?" I asked. A crucial part of this battle lay in knowing exactly when to retreat. We all knew our chances of winning the war here were extremely slim.

Ceph shook his head. "I can't really say. I'd guess a day, no more."

"I'll try and make it a little longer."

"May the Spirits guide you," he said stoically. "I'm just about to head down to my troops, we'll be needed soon."

"Then may the Spirits guide you too," I said, and we clasped hands before going our separate ways.

I found my men ready at the regroup point with

eleven new members, having been split off from other groups.

Captain Myra nodded to me. "Ready to draw some more blood?"

"Always."

She grinned. "I'll beat you this time."

"I hope you do."

"Then let's get to it." She raised her voice to the other troop leaders: "Secondary tunnels, now! Keep your march steady and once you reach the end, count to a hundred, then go."

We all moved out, keeping time with the steady marching of our feet. That was how we'd coordinate our attack.

My stomach tightened, though not for myself. I had been through far worse than this at Dwa Brody. I feared for my soldiers. The many men and women under me, some of whom would not see the end of this day. I couldn't think of that now though. They weren't dead yet, and before they went, hopefully they'd take many more of the enemy with them.

You care deeply for your men, don't you? Iomu asked.

I do. But it was more than that. *I know I can survive a lot and do a lot of damage. I worry that my men will try to be like me. Yet, they don't have my defenses, my strength and if they try to stand with me, it will only get them killed. Instead, I pray they will do their best today and live.*

I sensed Iomu's nod at this.

Before I entered the tunnel, I looked up at the blue

sky above me. There, an aerial battle was being waged, dragons fighting dragons.

Hard as my job was... I didn't envy Lyran this day.

"May the Spirits guide you too," I whispered for my friend. Then I entered the tunnel and my mind turned to the fight ahead of me.

CHAPTER 13

LYRAN

By the Sacred Fire, Ensar had done it!

He and his dragon Nolvinaran had used their powers and opened a massive portal to The Void, which had swallowed up Mesik, Nurgul, and Okan, and their dragons. They'd vanished in an instant, and Ensar had joined me as our other brothers had realized their betrayal. That left the odds at five on two, which were far better than I had been expecting. And with Eophon now far superior to what he had been when my brothers had known him long ago... Ensar and I might just have a chance.

Nolvinaran swung around to fly next to me, and Ensar called out: "Well met, brother!"

"Well met indeed! Shall we teach our siblings a lesson in humility?"

Ensar grinned. "We shall!" He spun several spheres of The Void around them. Eophon and I used our ability to vanish against the sky. And I knew just who my first target would be. I hadn't been there when Demir had forced himself on Roo. She had already made him pay for that, but I had my own score to settle.

We swept in, unseen, toward the little troll and his dragon Vastiphan.

Ready friend? I asked Eophon

Always.

The blast of fire caught my fat little brother straight on, not only severely burning him, but pushing him up and out of his dragon saddle. As the little troll fell, Eophon passed straight over Vastiphan's head, reaching down with their now-enhanced-and-stronger claws to tear through the other dragon's neck.

Dragon and rider fell from the sky, both would be dead when they hit the ground, if not before.

But then I saw Burak and his dragon Uthargan, swooping down to help. Burak's power was healing. If he could catch Demir and heal Vastiphan, the two would be up and about soon enough. I couldn't allow that, so I dove for them.

Even though I was still hidden, I felt a flash of awareness and knew someone else was close by.

Hakan and Atavashti approach, Eophon said. *With their power over wind and weather they may be able to sense our flight and target us with their lightning.*

We're faster, outdistance them, quick! I urged in haste.

Eophon dove almost straight down, quickly catching up to the falling Demir. But Burak was not far away behind us and Hakan, though still distant, would close swiftly as soon as we engaged with Burak.

We need to end this fight quickly.

That is unlikely given Burak and Uthargan's healing ability. They can recover from even the most severe wounds, probably even dragon-fire.

Eophon was right.

Blasted Pits! Apparently having lived with Dawn, Roo, and the others I'd picked up a few of their swear words.

Then here's the plan, wound them enough that they'll have to spend a moment healing themselves and won't be able to save Demir and Vastiphan. Then go deal with Hakan quickly and return to finish off Burak.

You have great faith in our abilities.

I do. We can do this!

Eophon was suspiciously quiet. I sensed their uncertainty. Still, we shifted slightly in our dive to bring us quickly over to Burak before he could reach Demir.

Give it everything you've got! I said drawing out a long javelin from the casing beside my dragon saddle. We closed quickly and at the last moment Burak shifted his gaze.

I'd forgotten, with his healing ability he could sense physical beings around him. But I hoped it would be too late for him.

I threw my javelin, and it took him high in his stomach, piercing his thick armor. Then Eophon's fire hit him and Uthargan. Eophon's claws were next, raking and tearing along Uthargan's flanks.

I heard the cry of my brother and the clash of his halberd on Eophon's hide

Are you well?

Yes, I am tougher now than I was before; hardly a scratch.

As we pulled away, I looked back. Eophon's fire had incinerated my javelin and Burak was charred and smoking, but still sitting in his saddle, halberd in hand. Yet, even as I glanced back, I saw some of his skin return to normal, healed and the heavy rips along Uthargan's flanks began to mend.

Pits! It wasn't enough.

And if we made another pass, Hakan would be upon us. But we didn't have a choice. We had to stop Burak from reaching Demir. Just a little longer and the little troll would hit the ground and be dead for certain.

Back! I commanded Eophon and he spun a tight turn. Luckily, we were smaller and faster than Uthargan and caught up quickly. But Burak was diving fast and closing in on Demir.

Blast him!

Eophon let out a constant stream of fire from behind Uthargan, burning Burak more and more. Uthargan's tail came up swishing around wildly and caught Eophon a nasty blow to their neck, which sent us reeling to one side.

Eophon! I shouted to them.

I am well... enough. But I felt the strain in their mental voice. *And I think we did it!*

Burak was limp in his saddle. I didn't know if he was

dead or not. Uthargan was hale enough though and still diving for Demir and Vastiphan, more toward the dragon than the man.

Demir hit the ground and bounced, shattered, dead.

But Uthargan got close enough that... Vastiphan seemed to come to life and spread their wings with enough time to buzz by the ground so low they knocked over men fighting, but then they were rising again.

Lightning blasted so close by me I felt the heat and crackling energy singeing my cheek.

Hakan had arrived. He couldn't quite determine where Eophon and I were, but that strike had been far too close for my liking.

Pits! I'd defeated one brother, but his dragon was still in the fight. And I was in a bad position, with Hakan closing, Burak healing and three dragons nearby.

Then, a black ball of void opened in front of the still diving Uthargan, just large enough for the beast's head and neck. Moving too fast to adjust course, Uthargan flew right into the void as it closed taking most of the front of the dragon with it, including Burak's legs and saddle. The burned man and what remained of his dragon fell from the sky, far too low now to get any help. The massive impact of the dragon's body sent men and earth flying.

Finish them! I commanded Eophon. I didn't think it likely that Uthargan would be able to heal, not without his head, but I didn't want to risk it.

Gladly.

We dove and blasted fire on the limp dragon form.

Eophon even landed, sinking claws deep into Uthargan, rending and tearing for a brief moment before quickly taking off again... just as lightning blasted down upon us. Some of it hit Eophon's flank, but most hit Uthargan.

I thanked Ensar for his help and looked up to see how he was doing, but as soon as I saw him, my heart fell.

He'd known Burak was by far one of the most dangerous of our brothers. The ability to heal any and all of the rest of them couldn't be allowed to linger. So, he'd gone after him, but that had left him open to attacks by Ati Kaan and Bayar. Nolvinaran had taken most of the blasts from Bayar, who wielded fire as his dragon-gift and the dragon wasn't looking well at all. Even as I watched, Vastiphan closed in and Nolvinaran and Ensar both seemed to freeze, tense and twitching. Demir's dragon was hitting them with pain.

Lightning blasted behind me. Again, too close for my liking. I couldn't forget about Hakan. But Ensar was falling from his dragon saddle and Nolvinaran was limp, falling as well. I had to save my brother who had sacrificed so much to help me!

Eophon sensed my thought and surged upward and over toward Ensar. We came under him and dove, matching his speed, before I plucked him from the sky, holding the large man close. But with Ensar in my lap, I'd not be able to fight.

Get us out of here!

Yes, I'm... sorry Lyran. I sensed Eophon's sorrow. They'd wanted to do more, to have inflicted greater damage upon their evil brethren. They'd thought their now superior form would have kept them in the fight longer. And in truth it might have. But we'd been outflanked,

Not your fault. Let's live to kill more of these bastards and beasts another day!

We sped away, faster than any of the other dragons except for maybe Hakan and Atavashti, but they didn't pursue. Now that I was gone, they could focus on our ground forces.

And I knew then, the battle would quickly turn in favor of our foes. Two million men were one thing, but adding in four dragons would quickly make the situation untenable.

I needed to drop Ensar off quickly, then return to harry my brothers and keep them from our troops.

Our troops? Eophon asked with faint amusement.

It was true. I had men who followed me down there, but mostly those below were men and women I'd never met from nations I'd never been to. But... I did feel connected to them. I was connected to Roo and Dawn, and they were in turn connected to these others, so I was too. These were my people now, not the Thraians.

And I had to protect them.

I directed Eophon to land behind our lines and gave Ensar over to the care of healers before quickly remounting.

Are you ready to face them? I asked my dearest friend.

We do what we must. We'll distract them for as long as we can.

Indeed, we shall. Let's go!

We leapt into the air and were quickly winging back toward my once-brothers. I'd keep them from the ground troops for as long as I could. I just hoped I'd survive this day to return to the women I loved.

CHAPTER 14

PAN

The Fey were fierce as they waded into the Thraian horde. Those with powers over metal, like me, reached out to heat and melt the armor off the enemy. The Thraians screamed as they burned from that which should have protected them. The Fey with power over wood and plants sprouted roots to trip and entwine our foes, while others — like the powerful and enigmatic Ahmaia — used the grasping cloth of their clothes to capture hundreds of men. Others, who worked earth itself, caused massive slabs to rise and slam together, killing dozens, or created pitfalls then closed them over, trapping men. It was the earth wielders who had burrowed the tunnels to get us this deep behind the enemy lines. Finally, there were a few Fey with us who worked with living beings themselves. Most of this type had remained behind the lines as healers. But a few had come with us.

They were clumped in the middle of our numbers, their mission to sap the strength of the enemy then push it back out to their allies.

It was a slaughter. The enemy had probably never seen anything like the Fey before.

And neither had Eona. She gasped and let out sounds of stunned wonder within me as she watched the wild and supernatural display. *I never knew...* she breathed.

Indeed. *Few people do. This is the true power of the Fey.*

Amazing.

And horrible.

That too.

Then fire, like the hottest forges, blasted down upon us. It burned Fey and Thraian alike in a massive line of destruction as a dragon swooped lower over us. Our time had run out.

"Retreat!" I called and the command was echoed out to the others. The earth-wielders immediately sucked the rest of us down to safety, though it was a horrid trip through loose earth to get to the cave which had been prepared below us. We all came out choking and sputtering, but we were safe now.

I sighed. Ensar and Lyran were supposed to have occupied the dragon lords longer, but in truth, I hadn't expected much from them. They had an impossible mission, far outnumbered.

I rose and steadied myself, finding my breath again as the earth shook and I fell once more. I'd forgotten about this part of the plan. Our earth-wielders were tearing the very battle-field asunder, breaking it in two, creating a chasm the enemy would not be able to cross quickly or easily. The savage thing about it was, we were deep within the enemy lines and hundreds-of-thousands of the enemy would be caught on our side of the divide, cut off from the rest of their army, with no support. They'd be slaughtered.

Then we would retreat.

But that was for those on the surface to do, not us Fey. We'd done our part in this battle. And we slowly made our way back through tunnels to the areas behind our lines.

I separated from the Fey as we emerged, going to find my friends.

Rhino found me, he was coming out from a different tunnel, covered in blood, looking like a terror from some nightmare, massive and fierce.

Spirits, but he's huge! Eona breathed. It didn't help that I was very short compared to the large man. He was a chest and shoulders and head taller than me. *And with that blood upon him, such a fearsome sight!*

I couldn't deny that.

"I need to get back out there to finish off the ones on our side of the divide, but... good work Pan." Rhino smiled down at me.

"It wasn't me." I hadn't created the divide. I hadn't even been able to control metal like the masters who'd melted the armor of our foes. I just fought with blade and fury.

"But you were commanding the Fey."

"Not so much commanding as... liaising with." They had their own commanders.

"Whatever. That new canyon out there is amazing, pass that on to whoever. Now, if you'll excuse me, I have to go kill some people."

"Have you heard from the others?" I asked quickly before he left.

"Ceph's troops are fully engaged, cleaning up what the Vauphani heavy cavalry and Njorvasoturi leave behind. Swift and Falcon are back with the healers, they're not wounded themselves, but a small force of Thraians got up into their archers' nest... and one of the dragons hit them too, I think. They have a lot of wounded. I haven't heard from Lyran." He looked skyward. I followed his gaze.

There was a swirl of dragons above, four of them. One or two might occasionally break off to attack ground troops, but something else was keeping them occupied. We couldn't see Lyran, but he was up there.

And suddenly I didn't want to just rest here. I needed to do more to help my valiant brothers. The Fey's part in this battle was done. I wasn't needed with them, so...

"I'm going with you," I said quickly drawing my sword. I felt like I'd done so little compared to the other Fey and I wanted to fight alongside a friend and make a difference today.

Rhino raised a bloody-brow but didn't argue. "Glad to have you. This way."

I'm proud of you Pan, so brave. Eona gave the impression of a reassuring hand on my shoulder. *Do what you can.*

Down another tunnel I went, and back out into the death and chaos of battle.

I fought beside Rhino... though not too close, as that long sword of his cleaved through foe and earth alike. I kept my distance from him and laid into the enemy troops. Blades bounced off me or shattered when they hit me. I was tougher now than when I'd fought Aaghar, my skin impenetrable. I may not be able to slay enemies as quickly as Rhino, but I'd last longer than anyone else on this battlefield.

This time... Rhino and I did not retreat to our tunnel. At this point the battle was decided and we had but one job, to finish off the enemy on this side of the crevice. It was gruesome, horrid work, but we could give no quarter, show no mercy. We didn't have the facilities to imprison so many men and we couldn't have them rejoining their army for the next fight. As gruesome as it was, we had to slay all the enemy who remained.

And by the time the sun was setting on that one day, as we all staggered, exhausted back to our camp, we had done it.

Our forces had taken out many times their number of the enemy. Rhino and I had tried to keep a tally just between us, but we'd both lost count.

I wasn't surprised to learn — several days later — that we'd destroyed almost a third of the massive Thraian army, close to seven hundred thousand men. But the toll to our side had been great as well. We'd lost roughly a quarter of our forces.

At this rate, neither side would win. We'd kill each other off, and Death itself would be the only victor.

But that wasn't entirely true. The armies might kill each other off, but the good citizens of Elista and the east would be saved from being conquered. That was what mattered, and it would be something worth fighting for... even if our army was destroyed to achieve it.

It wasn't a particularly pleasant thought for us in the army though. I sensed that the men around me knew it. They were quiet, heavy-hearted, as we marched to our next battlefield. I sensed the question on their minds: even if we stopped the enemy, would any of us be left alive to celebrate that victory?

My own heart was heavy until Fin came to find me, taking me back to the capital and a visit with Dawn in the realm of spirit. But when our two spirit forms — residual images of ourselves — met, I just fell into her arms, tired and drained. She held me close for a long time and I knew she was connecting with Roo, as my emotions slowly settled. She didn't ask how it had been. She knew war was bloody and awful. She just held me close.

It can't go on like this, I whispered. *We may win, but the cost will be too high.*

Then we need a new plan, don't we? she said softly. *And I think I know exactly what it should be.* She didn't say anything of her plan right then though, instead asking: *How far away are the others? When can we all be together again? I think, with the eight of us, we can end this war once and for all.*

If your mother allows it, I said heavily.

I love my mother, but she did what she wanted when she was my age, and I'll do the same.

I had to laugh a little at her stalwart determination to break rules.

The others should be here in a day or two, but I'm sure we could convince Fin to bring them sooner.

I don't want to risk tipping Fin off. He might tell mother we're up to something. It can wait a day or two. And until then, rest. Rest until you're strong enough to ravish me. Then ravish me until you need to rest.

That sounded like an excellent idea to me and suddenly, I was feeling enough strength and emotional fortitude to begin some of that ravishing. I turned toward her and pressed my lips to hers, tasting the sweet softness of their fullness against mine. Then, accessing my spirit-gift — well, Ceph's gift, which I still possessed — I sent tendrils of shivering bliss coursing through every part of Dawn's small frame. I spread my essence around her, caressing every part of her, inside and out, until she was a panting, screaming, puddle of pleasure. I didn't have the strength for more than one round with her, and soon I was expelled from the realm of spirit and back into my body to rest.

I just hoped, as I fell into a restful sleep, that whatever Dawn had planned would actually end this war without the need for both sides to slaughter themselves.

If she could do that, she'd prove herself to be every bit as amazing as I already believed her to be.

CHAPTER 15

ROO

DAWN'S PLAN WAS SIMPLE: KILL THE DRAGON LORDS AND cut the head off the snake. With no leaders, hopefully the army would surrender or at least disband and go home.

"And what does the queen think of your plan?" Ceph asked. He already knew the answer but wanted to hear us say it.

"She doesn't know," Dawn said, in control of my body at the moment.

Ceph nodded.

"They are cunning and dangerous foes," Lyran said softly. He knew firsthand. He and Eophon had barely survived their encounter with his brothers. They'd escaped only because of their ability to hide themselves. When he'd returned, he'd been next to death, but Ceph and Pan had patched him up. "Even with all of us against just them, it would be a tough fight. And it won't be just them. They'll have their most elite warriors guarding them, not to mention their dragons. It won't be easy to get near them."

"What if we went underground?" Pan asked. "I might be able to convince my cousin, an earth Fey, to help get us there."

Lyran tilted his head considering. "That would get us close. But still, if the fight drew out, there would be reinforcements there to help them soon enough."

"Which princes are left?" Falcon asked.

"And what are their powers?" Swift added.

"Three of my brothers and four dragons remain." Lyran sighed. "Bayar can summon fire, even without his dragon. And not just any fire, but the hottest flames, and he can target them very well. I once saw him summon fire *within* a person and he smiled as they screamed, burned from the inside out. He is dangerous, but the least dangerous of the three remaining."

"Hakan can summon lightning and control winds and weather. He can catch you up in a whirlwind as binding as steel, holding you aloft while he sucks the air from your lungs. Then just before you die from suffocation, he'll scorch you with lightning."

"Then, there's Ati Kaan, though from what Roo's told me, my eldest brother is pretty much The Kaan now. His powers are far more insidious. He'll toy with your mind, scooping out your deepest secrets and playing them out before your eyes as very convincing illusions as he shreds your sanity. He can also project bolts of pure mental energy, which do not do much damage, but will stun you. And while you stand there, he'll carve you to pieces with his swords."

"A pleasant group," Rhino grumbled.

"Indeed." Lyran sighed.

"How is Ensar doing?" Ceph asked. "Can he help us?"

Lyran shook his head. "Not only was he hurt badly when he switched sides, but he lost his dragon, and that wound is one of the soul. He mourns, but not in a way you can see. For now, he is insensate, unmoving, unseeing. It will be some time before he regains himself. And I do not think we have that sort of time. Still—" Lyran sighed. "He did more for our cause than any, taking four of my brothers out of the fight. If not for him, then what Dawn proposes now would be impossible instead of just suicidal."

"He's done enough," Dawn added. "So... are you all in? Will you go with me to—"

"With you?" Pan piped up quickly. "You plan to go yourself?"

"Am I not a better warrior than you?" Dawn challenged the Fey.

He grimaced and mumbled something which sounded like "Well... yes, but... still."

"I'm tired of being cooped up in here," Dawn said. And I knew she meant 'in the palace' as well as 'in this body.' I tried not to take offence.

"You are indeed a bold and brave warrior," Lyran said. "But you are not practiced in fighting in this current form. Roo's body isn't as fast nor agile as yours. She is graceful and lithe, yes, but not on the same level as your previous form."

It was true. I liked to think I was smooth and flowing in my movements, and compared to many women I may have been, but compared to Dawn... I was a lumbering lump.

And Dawn knew it too.

She'd been experimenting, moving through forms and practice fighting in my body, and even I could sense she wanted to be smoother and faster and more precise than this body would allow.

"Roo and I are far from useless. I can protect us well enough physically and together, with our power over spirit and emotions, we can be devastating. You've all seen what we can do."

The men nodded to this, but I could still see the hesitancy on their faces. In truth, I was hesitant as well. I didn't like being in the thick of combat.

I'll protect you, Dawn said within me, sensing my hesitation.

As will I, Leoa added.

And I, Amya chimed in.

I was host to all of them and they knew if I died it would be the end of myself and Dawn and a very sad parting for Leoa and Amya.

Thank you, all, I said and meant it. Though I still

worried that my larger form would hinder Dawn in her attempts to fight.

Outwardly, Dawn raged on: "And don't even one of you dare say anything about losing me. When you all go off to fight, do I make any big fuss about losing you? No. I know you're all capable and will do everything in your power to stay alive and return to me, to us. So, if it's not about that, then what? Why don't you want me to go?"

"What about Roo?" Ceph asked. "Does she want to go? You are in her body." He gave a half-grin. "Can I make a fuss about losing her?"

"You can, but it won't help," Dawn said quickly, glaring at him.

He's not wrong, I said. *I am the sort to make a fuss, to worry and fret about my lovers being off at the front lines. And if it were me alone, I know they would worry for me too.*

But it's not you alone, Dawn countered. She knew that if we did this, she'd be dragging me along for the fight. I had made peace with this — Dawn and I had discussed this at length before now — but it didn't mean I liked it.

I know. I'd say no more on it.

"What if we can separate the two of them?" Pan asked. He and Ceph shared a long look.

"Have you figured out how?" Dawn asked.

I was very curious as well.

"The theory we have is sound," Ceph said slowly. "But... nothing like this has ever been done before, we have no clue if it will work."

Dawn and I were on the same page when she asked: "What does it involve?"

Ceph again shared a long look at Pan, then spoke. "Well, from what you've told us, the only reason you were able to bond with Roo and inhabit her body was because you already had a connection with her. Hence, from what we can tell, the requirements to get you back into your own body would be—" He held up one finger. "—To have a body." Another finger. "To be able to connect with it to get your spirit inside it." He looked at Pan and the other man nodded. "We believe we can create a new body from scratch. It will not be easy at all, but we think it's doable. The trouble would be... there would be no spirit within it for you to connect to. You'd have no way to get your spirit into that body. That is unless..." We all hung on his words as he paused for a breath. "We take a bit of Roo herself to start the process of creating the new body, that way you'd already be *in* the body, at least partially, and could inhabit it once we were finished. Still, the process would be... painful for Roo and probably extremely difficult and potentially dangerous for you." Dawn was about to speak, but Ceph pushed on. "Also, again, we think we know the theory of how we would create a new body from Roo's, but... we don't actually know what the end result would be, if it would truly be the same as your previous body, Dawn. There is a good chance it would be... different and we don't know exactly how."

Pan picked up quickly, probably seeing the distress and concern Dawn was showing on my face. "Before you... before you died, we had both healed you enough times to know the feel of your body. We believe we can take any tissue and eventually make it as you had been, but it may take a bit of time and some additional work after the initial transition to get it just right. But Ceph's ability is the perfect tool to do this and with the two of us working together, we believe it is possible."

"Possible yes, but still dangerous and painful," Ceph added.

"Then do it, now," Dawn demanded.

Are you sure? I was a bit shocked. I wasn't looking forward to the "painful" part.

I love you Roo, but we both know the sooner I'm out of here, the better for both of us. This has been an interesting and informative experience, but I'm not meant to be here.

I couldn't deny that.

"We'll need some time to prepare, and so will you. We'll all want to be well rested for this. All of us." Pan motioned to the four other men. "We'll want you to be linked with Dawn in spirit to help give her and us strength to do this."

They all nodded.

"If we get a good rest tonight, perhaps we can try tomorrow," Ceph said.

I felt Dawn's mischief and desire spike. "And one way to ensure we all get a good rest is to tire you all out." She reached out to spirit link with each of them.

Oh... we're doing this again? Now? I asked. Not that I minded.

Might as well get ourselves all loose and worked up, have one last hurrah before we go our separate ways.

I felt my desire build in anticipation of what was to come. *Ooooh, sounds good to me,* I said, filled with bubbling emotion. I too reached out to the men and felt their individual yearning.

"Strip." Dawn's hard command in my voice send thrills through the gathered men.

"Are we doing this in spirit?" Rhino asked, quickly disrobing.

"Partly, yes, but I've been wanting to try something else." That got their attention... and mine. My heat spiked as I recalled Dawn telling me of her fantasy. "I want all six of you pleasuring this one body, all at the same time."

That got a lot of curious and heated glances.

Are you well with this? Dawn asked me. It was my body after all.

Part of me was terrified, but only a small part, the rest was excited and curious. *Yes, let's do it!*

I felt a thrill run through Dawn as she discarded the silken wrap we'd been wearing. She went to the bed, hopping up to sit on the side opening my legs.

"I'm gonna need to be really wet and loose for this to work, so who wants to get me worked up?"

There was no shortage of volunteers. In the end, they all contributed.

This is the easy part. Mind if I take control for a while? You can take things back once we move on to the next bit.

Yeah, go ahead.

Dawn and I switched. And I came fully into my physical senses. A warm breeze from the open window brushed over my body, sending shivers through me. I felt the silken sheets and soft bed beneath me smooth against my legs. More than that, was the intense heat of my body, the roiling, molten desire deep in my core. My folds were already slick with anticipation of what was to come, my nipples half-aroused. As my chest rose with heavy breaths.

My men came to me.

Rhino knelt beside the bed and began kissing up my inner thigh until his lips pressed softly to my folds. Then his tongue darted out to wet me and he began his oral ministrations in earnest.

The twins climbed up next to me as I lay back. They took a side of me each and began kissing me all over, though most of their focus was upon my breasts. Soon enough my nipples were taut, my areolae flushed and swollen. Lyran was above me and leaned down to kiss my lips and face. Altogether I felt a wonderful and amazing sense of union and love.

Then Ceph and Pan, reaching out with their gifts, sent shivering thrills through my body, as if feathers were ever-so-lightly brushing over me. And soon enough I wanted more than just Rhino's tongue at my ready entrance.

Ceph took over, his cock, though long, was slender and he was easily inside me. But he didn't dip too far. He kept his thrusts shallow and with each slow push came tingles of electrified delight shocking through me. I moaned into Lyran's lips, trying to buck and sway upon Ceph's cock to draw him deeper. And when Ceph finally touched my deepest point, filling me, he sent a flash of physical delight through me. I shuddered with the hard-clenching shocks of a powerful orgasm, only enhanced by the caresses and kisses of the other men around me.

Harder, more, we need to be so very loose and wet, Dawn said within me. I lifted Lyran from my lips to gasp out the command verbatim.

Ceph obliged, instantly beginning a hard pounding of his erection inside me. I almost instantly had another thrilling peak, since he hadn't stopped his internal stimulation. The feel of his thrusts was utterly amazing! And after he'd made me come again, he moved and was replaced by Falcon.

Ceph moved to stroke and kiss my lower belly, over where Falcon drove himself within me. Ceph kept up his arousing touch, making Falcon's cock feel scintillatingly glorious inside me. I felt myself grow wetter and looser. Swift took over from Falcon, having his turn to drive deep and help me grow even more aroused and wet.

Then came Lyran, slightly thicker than the twins and definitely longer. I accepted him easily as he lunged hard within me. Ceph had moved his lips to my breasts, plucking at them with teeth and sending all manner of amazing sensations through me as his hand still stroked my belly.

Then finally Rhino was inside me, thicker still, longer

still, opening me to my limits — or so I thought — as he filled me and pounded just as hard as the others within my depths. And when that massive erection of his moved with ease into my flooded folds, I knew... I was ready for more.

CHAPTER 16

DAWN

My turn, I said, taking control of Roo's body as Rhino grunted, thrusting hard inside me. I'd been party to the rising desire and four and a half orgasms Roo had felt so far. Now, as I came into her senses fully and felt the massiveness of Rhino surging upon me, I myself was thrown into a hard, body-clenching orgasm.

Roo laughed, delighted and still tingling with her own bliss. I felt her rise to another peak as I did. And there would be more to come.

"Enough!" I cried out, and Rhino slowed to a stop but remained full and hard within me. Gods, he felt amazing!

"Falcon, lie on the bed beside me," I commanded, voice hoarse and raw.

The dark-skinned young man complied.

"Swift, get between his legs," I said as I nodded for Rhino to withdraw. He did, and for a moment I gasped at the gaping loss I felt. But I then grinned, knowing I'd be full enough soon.

I quickly rolled over onto Falcon and his cock easily slid inside me. It felt so small! "Are you ready for something fun?" I asked him, pressing Roo's lips to his. He nodded, clearly eager.

Swift was playing with my rear opening, but I called back to him. "No, get in my pussy with your brother!"

I felt his hesitation, even if I couldn't see him, but it didn't last long. I felt the tip of his erection trail down to my opening and slowly push in.

I saw Falcon's eyes go wide as he must have felt the second cock sliding alongside his own. "Oh!" he gasped. Yeah, I was sure that extra friction would do wonders for him and Swift. And for me...

Oh, indeed!

Rhino was big, yes, but the twins together, thick as their cocks were, stretched me even more. And suddenly I was so extremely tight around their twin erections, pressing incredibly deep inside me.

I didn't have words, I gasped and grunted and ground myself down upon them, wanting more. They were happy to oblige.

This... this was just the tip of the iceberg. But I couldn't find my voice to speak to the others. So, I slipped into spirit and reached out to Lyran.

Climb on top and get in my ass! I commanded him.

Oh spirits, here we go! Roo said, trembling with desire inside me.

This is going to be something new indeed, Amya added. Leoa purred with delight.

It took a moment for Lyran to do as I'd instructed. First there was oil which needed to be applied to me and him. Then Swift fingered me, to help get me open and ready. Lyran clambered on top of me, and Swift helped him to get in place before he began soft pushes to enter me from behind. And when I finally opened to him, accepting that long cock of his, feeling it slide deeper inside me. I cried out in utter bliss as these three cocks alone were driving me mad!

Through another spirit link I connected with Rhino and soon he was up on the bed kneeling next to my head. He gently tilted my head. Unable to speak — or do much more than whimper through one rising orgasm after another — I opened my lips to him and felt the thick shaft of his cock fill my mouth. I slid my tongue around this heavy tip as he stroked my hair and supported my head.

But I wasn't done yet. I reached out to Ceph and Pan. I had two hands and I wanted them full of man-meat. I was a bit too distracted by all the other — amazing and wonderful — sensations to reach them myself, but once they were in place. They found my hands and placed them upon their cocks, and I gripped and rubbed them furiously.

Pan hadn't been sure about this when I'd mentioned it to him during our time together before the others had arrived, but I'd convinced him he had to be a part of this, that he'd be helping me, his love, experience something... amazing! He'd relented. And he certainly seemed aroused enough now as I stroked his hard shaft.

Spirits! Roo breathed within me.

All of them, all our men, were seeking a single, mutual pleasure and making me insanely joyous.

Once they were all in place, I reached out and drew them into my spirit, connecting them with myself and Roo. Roo reached through me into their emotions and stroked their ecstasy.

Make them come, I whispered to Roo. *Make them all come at once!*

Roo drifted up to join me, such that, for a moment, we were together sharing access to her body; both feeling everything our men were doing to pleasure us.

Already the guys were trembling, thrusting all the harder as they felt their pleasure rise to a crescendo.

Here we go, Roo whispered and spiked their pleasure through the roof, making them feel what I was feeling.

And they all erupted as one.

The twins swelled to nearly painful lengths and released within me. Dual surges, pulsing in turn, to fill me. Lyran's hot flow unleashed a heavy pool of warmth deep within me. Rhino shuddered and roared as he filled my mouth — several times over — and I felt the hot streamers from Ceph and Pan upon my sides and arms and hands; a welcome mess.

And the moment drew out. The mingling of all their

desires within my spirit, lasted for a long and achingly amazing time.

Never before had I felt anything like this, the joining of all of us, physically *and* spiritually.

We parted slowly and carefully, and I was moved to a basin for washing. The top blanket of my bed was thrown into the hearth and burned as others bathed me, and themselves.

We gathered close that night, all huddled together upon the large bed in my room. I moved over them kissing them each in turn, once as me, once as Roo, a thank you and a promise.

Tomorrow we'd try to bring me back, build me a body and extricate me from Roo. Tomorrow I'd be myself again.

Or so I hoped... desperately.

CHAPTER 17

CEPH

Spirits, I hoped this worked. Roo and Dawn were relying on me to separate them, creating a new body for Dawn. This had to work.

I drew a deep breath and looked at Pan. He was stoic, still, ready. He nodded to me. This wasn't even his given spirit-gift, how could he be calmer and more prepared than I was? Though... I had lost my spirit gift for a while. Perhaps that was what plagued me. This would be another instance where I could potentially go too far and burn myself out. Though, with Pan helping that wasn't likely, but it was still possible. It all depended on how difficult this turned out to be.

Ceph... Ulio prodded within my mind.

Shut up, I need to concentrate.

What you're doing... no one has ever done anything like this before. It's...

Crazy? I don't need your pessimism right now, please go away!

I was going to say daring and exciting and ground-breaking.

Oh.

And, also, I know I can be a bit... superior at times, but for this, for you and the woman you love, and this life-altering task, I'm here for you, you have all my strength at your disposal.

I was more than a little shocked at Ulio's sacrifice and kindness. Though I suspected part of the Lumani's motivation to help was so they could be a part of this miracle and brag about it later.

Maybe, Ulio admitted freely.

That actually made me laugh internally. *Well, thanks anyway.*

"Ready?" I asked Roo. She lay, naked, to one side of the large bed.

She smiled up at me, raising a hand to my cheek. "I can sense your fear and uncertainty. Don't worry. I'll be well. I know you can do this. I'm ready."

She sent me a bit of calm and certainty through her touch, and I felt my tension drain away.

"Thank you," I whispered.

She let fall her arm and closed her eyes, then with one large breath, she too relaxed.

I looked at Pan again. He nodded.

"Begin," I said softly. Pan and I would be working

toward the same goal, but on different parts. I would be gathering "Excess" material from Roo and sending it to him. He would be drawing it out from her to create Dawn's body.

We had experimented with this a little to find out how much "excess" material there was within a person, and Pan and I had both been shocked at the answer. Basically, our bodies were constantly growing, tiny particles within us constantly splitting and creating a new body for us. At the same time, other particles were dying and being sloughed off. But the overall effect was that the body had an incredible ability to remake itself, and hence to potentially lose much of itself while remaining a full and healthy body. Though what we were about to do would be taking more than we should from Roo. It would be incredibly painful. She knew that and was prepared for it.

I started with the area where we were going to connect the two bodies. In order to create the second, we had to "grow" it from Roo. Hence, it had to be attached to her, at least for now. And we'd determined the safest place to have that happen was at her hip. I placed my hands there and dug deep within her, carefully selecting every excess bit of herself and sending it to the spot on her hip where Pan waited. A growth appeared, and Pan began to form it from there. He would build Dawn's new body as more and more of Roo was sent to him. He began by sculpting a mirrored hip.

Roo squirmed a little, drawing a breath. She was uncomfortable already, but this was just the beginning.

We worked for hours but couldn't stop. The other guys came with drinks and small bits of food we could eat, not just for Pan and me, but for Roo as well to keep up her strength. And Roo, for her part, was a stalwart warrior for the process. She wept and whimpered at the pain, tears leaking from her eyes, but rarely screamed in true agony. When she did, it sent a spike to my heart, but I had to keep going.

Dawn's body was nearly ready, nearly done. I looked up from my work at Pan and the body he was creating and instantly saw his exertion and consternation. He was dripping with sweat and... the body he was creating... wasn't right.

The size and shape were Dawn's, smaller and slimmer than Roo, but the skin wasn't Dawn's pale fairness, but Roo's dark honey tan. The eyes were Roo's sable, not Dawn's gold, and the hair was Roo's auburn, not Dawn's raven black. The shape was right, but the look was all wrong.

I couldn't stop, and speaking would be a distraction, but I had to ask: "Pan, are you well?"

"No," he whimpered. "I can't... It won't..."

This wasn't working.

I swore internally. We'd erred somewhere, and I didn't know how to fix this, not while I was concentrating on not tearing Roo apart.

"We'll undo it for now, we need to stop and put it all

back. We... need more time, more information."

Pan nodded, tears falling from his eyes, jaw tight.

Luckily, the process of putting everything back into Roo was far easier and quicker than extracting it to begin with. That was much like the healing I did normally. Still, we were careful and took our time.

The sun was low in the sky by the time we'd finished, and Pan and I collapsed in exhaustion. Roo wept openly, though I don't know if it was Roo or Dawn doing the crying. They knew we'd failed.

The others drew close, comforting all of us.

"What happened?" Rhino asked softly.

"I don't know!" I snapped at him. "It... we didn't..." I shook my head and broke down into tears.

Pan and I were placed on the bed beside Roo and the three of us rested and sobbed together as the others did their best to soothe us and get us whatever we needed.

It was Roo who — unsurprisingly — found her emotional core first. She asked the others to leave the room and sent calm into myself and Pan. We settled after a moment.

"I... I won't ask what happened," she said, her voice still raw from the pain and weeping she'd been experiencing nearly all day. "But I know you two can do this. I won't ask you to do it again, not until you're ready. Take the time you need. Dawn and I will be well for now.

"I'm so sorry," Pan whispered, and I knew he wasn't speaking to Roo.

Roo shifted and the voice that spoke next wasn't hers.

Still, it was strained and there was a deep and clenching pain in it. "I know Pan, my love, I know. You and Ceph will figure this out and get me a body. Just... not today, and not before we take care of the Thraians. That can't wait any longer and I think... we were all under too much pressure to succeed this time." She swallowed hard and I could tell she was keeping back tears. "We are strong, and all of us are stronger together. We will defeat the Thraians, then figure this out."

Pan nodded, unable to speak. He closed his eyes and kissed her softly, flinching just a little at the touch. I felt for the man. I still had the body of the woman I loved here to touch and feel but he didn't, and every kiss must have felt wrong to him.

We rested and regained our strength for several days. Luckily, we had time. It took two weeks for the massive Thraian army to cross Elista and set up camp across the vast field of battle we'd prepared for them.

Pan and I studied and worked, learning, and growing our skill, but still didn't feel comfortable to try the separation again before the time came for Dawn's plan to be enacted.

The night came; the night we would hopefully end this war once and for all.

But I felt a hint of doubt. I had so wanted to help Dawn and Roo, but we'd not been able to. That failure still clung to me like a leech.

But Roo was ready, as was Dawn. They would lead us.

We prepared for battle, then snuck out of the estate to

meet Pan's earth Fey cousin. A tunnel had already been started and we slipped quietly below the earth into deeper darkness. A lantern was lit and shed swaying light upon the soft earthen walls as we set off in silence.

This was it.

To fail now... meant death.

CHAPTER 18

PAN

I'D FAILED.

It had been up to me to form Dawn's new body. I was the one with a perfect memory of what she should be, from the many times I'd used Ceph's power to heal her. But... something had gone wrong. I'd been concentrating on that pale face, the wild grin and those sparkling golden eyes, like a new day's sunrise. I'd had the image perfect in my mind, but... it hadn't translated to the form. And the harder I'd tried, the worse I'd felt and the harder the entire process had become. I'd been at the end of my strength, with my mind reeling by the time Ceph had noticed and told me to stop.

I'd failed.

And Dawn was still trapped, distant from me. Even though I felt her, close to my heart, a part of my spirit. I couldn't touch her and that tore at my soul. I was ready to tear apart these dragon lords with the rage I felt inside.

Rage at myself, that I was more than ready to take out on someone.

Pan, you did the best you could, and you've learned more since then. This will work eventually, I know it! Eona was trying to lift my spirits and failing. *You need to be calm now. Fighting with such rage in your heart can make you foolish and reckless. I can help you—*

I don't want to be calm, right now, Eona. Just let me have this, let me take out all my frustrations on these bastards.

I sensed Eona's concern. *As you wish Pan. I'll try to keep you safe, where I can.*

I hissed a scornful laugh at that. *I'm invincible now, there's no need for me to hold back.*

Still, I felt her uncertainty.

I pushed her away and focused on the battle ahead.

Pendryl, my earth Fey cousin, stopped ahead of me. "This is the end," he said softly. "From everything I've gathered, the area of the enemy camp reserved for the commanders is directly above us. We're below a pavilion housing one of the dragon lords. I've created tunnels to the other two pavilions as well." He pointed at two other tunnels. "I'll wait for you here. Once you've dealt with the dragon lord above, return and I'll take you to the others."

"Thank you," I whispered to him. "If... if things go badly, if we don't return, collapse these tunnels and return to the others."

Pendryl nodded. "I'm sure, you'll do well, Eadric," he said using my former Fey name. "But... I will do as you command."

Good. I nodded to him. "How do we get up?"

Pendryl gave a half-smile. "The hard way."

I hated the hard way: being pushed up through the earth forcibly, having the soil moved around you.

"When you're ready to return, one of you stamp hard on the ground five times."

I nodded.

The others were gathered close, ready.

"The one above us is peaceful, resting. I don't know if they're asleep, but they're not active," Roo said softly. "There are two others close by, probably guards, and another four not far away." She looked up at us. "Shall I make them empty, try to put them to sleep? If it doesn't work, they'll be warned of something happening."

"Why don't we wait until we're up there," Lyran said softly, sword out and ready.

The others nodded.

"Are we good?" I asked.

More nods.

"Stand here," Pendryl said pointing.

We gathered close, holding hands to keep us together.

Then it came, the earth pushing us up and into more soil. The ground pressed around me, but Pendryl was at least good at keeping the dust and dirt from getting too close to our heads, so when we popped out at the top, we weren't sputtering or coughing.

We all kept still for a long moment, waiting and listening. Had the movement of the earth alerted anyone?

All seemed quiet.

No one stirred.

I began to breathe a sigh of relief...

When soft laughter greeted my ears.

Then came clapping, not loud, but in the silence it seemed each slap of the hands was a war-cry or shout for alarm!

"Well done," A deep voice said softly.

"Pits," Roo and Lyran swore at once.

Lyran continued with: "Kaan."

So, we'd been unlucky enough to find the nastiest of the dragon lords first.

"I see you've brought me some toys to play with, little brother." The voice issued out from deeper in the darkness of the large pavilion. "And... the same delicious young woman who came to my capital and castrated one of our brothers. I'll be sure to keep her alive after I've killed the rest of you. She deserves a slow and painful death." And his tone suggested he was eagerly looking forward to that.

Roo has taken care of the guards. Dawn spoke into our spirits, through the indelible link we'd all formed.

Don't underestimate Kaan, he alone will be a formidable challenge. Lyran's warning was not needed. He'd already prepared us for this.

Let's do this! Falcon said eager for a fight.

Kaan laughed again and soft footfalls drew closer as a heavy partition of the pavilion was moved aside. "Since you're all so eager for a fight, by all means, *fight*." There was something in how he said the last word which ran through my mind and pushed upon me: a command. I don't know why I wasn't affected, perhaps because I was Fey. Lyran was also immune, it seemed. Roo and Dawn were two souls in one, two minds in one, and were able to resist him, but the others...

Swords clashed and voices roared as Falcon, Swift, Rhino, and Ceph all began fighting each other. And this was no play-fighting. They meant to kill.

Kaan laughed a much deeper and fuller sound. "Too easy."

"I'm still here brother!" Lyran said, launching himself forward to engage his older brother. Yet, it quickly became apparent that Kaan was the vastly superior swordsman. He was older by nearly twenty years and far more experienced. And his dragon-link had kept him young and strong. Even when Lyran went unseen, Kaan only laughed. He'd know where his brother's mind was and what he planned. There would be no hiding from the man.

Lyran was outmatched.

That left me divided. Should I help Lyran or try to stop the others from killing each other?

Go, help Lyran, I'll take care of the rest, Dawn said within me.

That was all I needed. I had a target for my rage, and I darted forward to let it all out.

I wasn't the swordsman Lyran was, but I was determined and... I was very hard to hurt or kill. I'd been hit by Aaghar's blade and survived, and though Kaan's sword was faster and more precise, he did not have the strength of Aaghar and the many hits upon me simply skidded off my unnaturally tough skin, shredding my clothes.

"You're a tough one, aren't you? Have I even damaged you?" Kaan seemed impressed, but he wasn't winded yet, nor did he sound worried.

That's when I felt it, a blast from nowhere, which struck more mentally than physically. I staggered back a step; my thoughts scattered to the four winds. For a long moment I didn't even know who I was, or where I was, or what was happening. Slowly parts of me began to reassemble and my thoughts reformed. That must have been Kaan's stunning mental blast. I hadn't been prepared for it at all.

Kaan hadn't attacked me while I was out. He'd been focusing all his efforts on his brother and Lyran was flagging, bleeding from a dozen wounds, a couple of which were nasty.

I plucked up my sword and rose slowly.

I knew fighting Kaan was useless. He was too good and too fast. I'd not land a hit... but I could help Lyran; heal him. I took a step forward toward my comrade... when a blast of lightning exploded into the pavilion and hammered down upon me.

All I saw was a blinding light as my body convulsed with a power it could not contain. I think I screamed. I know I fell.

I lay, smoldering, smelling the sickening scent of my own charred flesh. But... I wasn't out of the fight. I rose slowly, trying to blink the spots — which wouldn't go away — from my vision as two new forms stormed into the pavilion.

And overhead, there came the heavy flap of dragon's wings.

Suddenly, this felt more and more like a trap than our intended ambush.

Fire erupted nearby and I flinched. I still clutched my sword, and I threw myself at one of the other brothers, in hopes of at least distracting them. I may have been burned, but I was made of tougher stuff than most. I could keep going, though... I didn't know for how long. All I knew was, I had to keep fighting to protect the others. I was one of the few not under Kaan's control. I had to do something.

My blade met another, which was suddenly engulphed in flames: Bayar.

"Hello little one," the large man said, sneering down at me. "Time for you to die."

We'd see about that.

CHAPTER 19

RHINO

EVERYONE WAS MY ENEMY!

This didn't make any sense. Why had I come here? I was hopelessly outnumbered. Who were these people? I had some sneaking suspicion something was wrong, perhaps I'd been lured here? I didn't know and I was just getting more and more angry about it.

Whoever these people were, they were quick. I was stronger, I was sure of that, but I was having trouble hitting the many foes around me.

Rhino! Please Stop!

And there was that voice again. It wasn't anyone I was fighting. The voice was a woman's, and these were all men. And I felt like I should know the woman who owned that voice. But I couldn't quite figure out who they were and why they wanted me to die, because surely if I stopped fighting, these others would quickly kill me.

Yes, Please Rhino, you need to listen to her!

This voice was different, still female but seemingly much closer. They almost felt like they were in my mind with me.

I dare not respond; dare not lose focus on my enemies.

They're not your enemies, you're being tricked! The second voice again. I still didn't fully trust her even though I felt I should.

Listen to her, Rhino, we're trying to help you! The first voice. This one didn't feel close and yet... it made my heart clench. I wanted to know it, I wanted to be near it. I had a visceral reaction to it, a heavy pull of love and desire.

Rhino, listen to me!

Who are you? I asked, careful not to take my attention off those around me.

You don't recognize me? Spirits! Kaan messed you up bad. It's Dawn, your beloved.

Dawn? Beloved? I should know that name. It meant something. But still... *I can't stop fighting or I'll die.*

What?

The second voice answered, clarifying: *He thinks everyone around him is an enemy, that they all want to kill him. He believes he's just trying to defend himself!*

Yes! I said. That voice had the gist of it.

Thanks, Iomu, that sheds some light on things. Roo, flood them with love, for us and each other. I'm going to try something at the same time.

Roo? That name also sounded like it should mean something.

Then my anger and fear and wariness were all smothered by an overwhelming feeling of love. I... suddenly loved everyone around me. Why would I have been fighting someone I loved? What had happened?

We all stopped fighting. The others seemed as disoriented as I was.

Then I was hit by another overpowering wave of... I didn't know what it was, but I felt intricately connected with those I'd been fighting.

And it was only then that I risked a moment to look around. There were others fighting. A tall man, though not as tall as I, was not doing well fighting against one who looked vaguely like him but older. A tiny man, who looked like he been badly burned, fought a man with a sword of flames. And — Blessed Spirits — there were dragons!

I didn't know what was happening, but I felt deeply connected with that tall man, and the short one, and... a woman. I turned to her, and it was only when my gaze landed on Roo, that everything flooded back to me.

I knew who everyone was, and why I was here. Just seeing Roo's amazing form was enough to jog my memory back to itself. Back from... Kaan's trickery.

The others snapped out of their reverie at the same time.

"Help them!" Roo shouted to us.

And we scattered.

Above us, two dragons peeled off to fight another which had just arrived: Eophon.

Good.

But still, we were in the middle of the enemy camp. The pavilion we'd been in had been destroyed and we fought mostly out in the open now against three dragon lords, four dragons, and more men arriving every moment.

Ceph went to help Lyran, healing him while adding his sword to the fight against Kaan. The twins ran to help Pan.

That left...

I didn't know the man by sight, but I guessed the dragon lord approaching me was Hakan. Lightning danced and crackled all around him. He smiled at me and raised his sword, which also shimmered with lightning.

I charged him with a roar and his smile grew. He braced for my attack, but at the last moment I veered into my avatar form and flew past him. I smiled inwardly at the shock on his face. Then, once I was behind him, I shifted back, spinning in mid-air to slash down at him. He was quick and already moving out of the way. So, instead of cleaving through his head, I sliced down through his shoulder and removed his sword arm.

Lightning raced up my sword and shocked through me, but I gritted through it and landed on both feet. I wanted to follow up with a killing blow, but Hakan burst forth with wind blasting myself — and everything else around him — away. I might have held my ground if it had been just the wind, but then bolts of lightning blasted at me, searing skin and throwing me dozens of feet. I landed hard on my back, the breath knocked out of me, agony burning where I'd been hit, but still I rose.

Hakan was suffering and struggling to recover, but I'd not be able to get back to him quickly. I'd been thrown clear of the fight and now had twenty or more men around me, all of whom were ready for a fight.

I roared and let myself sink into the semi-comforting thrill of battle. This was a fight I knew well, against a large number of foes. I veered into and out of my avatar form, flitting through them, swinging my heavy sword in wide strokes, slashing through two or three at a time. Still, there seemed to be no end to them. More and more came. I fought desperately, perhaps the best I'd ever fought. Yet these were no ordinary soldiers, but hardened campaigners, experienced veterans and a few of their hits got through, scoring me. Every cut, even if they weren't deep, only added pain to my already near-debilitating anguish from Hakan's lightning strike. I was starting to slow, growing sluggish when...

Suddenly there were no more men.

I'd broken through the tide.

Hundreds of men lay dead around me.

More were coming, I heard them in the night, charging toward me, but they weren't here yet and I had a moment to myself.

I looked back at Hakan. He had his sword in his other

hand now and lightning crackled over the stump of his wounded shoulder, cauterizing it. He was moving toward me slowly, hate and revenge in his eyes. Then his gaze — just for an instant — flicked up.

His dragon.

Iomu sensed it too. *Above you Rhino! Move!*

I dove as a massive blast of lightning hit where I had been, but I hadn't been quick enough. The strike had caught my left leg below the knee.

I screamed as I rolled and tried to come up standing, but I collapsed immediately. My left leg was useless now, a shriveled and smoking stump where my calf had been.

The dragon above me dove and I knew I'd be dead in an instant. I veered and dove for the ground, impacting hard as the snapping jaws and swiping claws passed through where I had been.

I pushed up from the ground and began flying, though the damage done to me had transferred to this form and my wings were weak. I bobbed and weaved heavily, like a drunkard. I needed to reach Hakan.

He was looking all around him. He knew I hadn't been swallowed up by his dragon.

I got close enough to strike, then flew above him and transformed back. My blow was awkward as I fell at him.

Again, he sensed me and shifted to one side, I caught a glancing blow to his leg and heard his cry. I gave a grim smile even as I hit the ground on my shoulder and side, my head bouncing hard off the packed earth.

I saw only stars, but I sensed Hakan was close enough

that a long slash of my sword might hit him, I lashed out blindly, but I felt nothing and heard the shifting metal of his armor as he moved.

He rolled away, coming to his feet. Get up, Rhino! Iomu luckily still had some sense, even as I began to regain my sight.

I carefully rose to my one good foot as my head cleared, still aching.

"Now you die," Hakan said with a sneer and again his shifting eyes gave away his dragon's location. I immediately veered and flew up as the jaws of a dragon snapped through where I had been. I veered back almost instantly, sword plunging down, driving my blade into the dragon's skull with all the power I possessed. I felt the resistance of scales and bone, then the satisfying crunch as those gave way and my massive sword plunged into the beast's brain.

The dragon died, but dragged me with it for several hundred feet, as it had been in flight, swooping low, when I'd killed it.

When we'd come to a full stop, I drew my blade out and veered to fly down off the massive form. Returning to myself, I used my sword to keep myself from falling.

That was pure badass, Rhino. Amazing! Iomu sounded almost euphoric.

Hakan was on his knees, eyes and mouth gaping at me and his dead dragon. I recalled something Lyran had said, about how the loss of a dragon was devastating for a dragon lord. It wouldn't kill them, but they'd probably go temporarily mad, or fall unconscious.

It seemed Hakan had chosen the "going mad" option. He was crackling with energy like nothing before and he looked like he was about to explode. And indeed, he did. Devastating winds and blasting lightning erupted from where he knelt and destroyed everything within a hundred feet of him. Then he collapsed.

I risked flying over to him now. He looked dazed or dead, unmoving. But I'd not risk his revival, so I removed his head for good measure.

Then, I went to help the others.

CHAPTER 20

SWIFT

I was exhausted but couldn't stop moving. To stop was to die. Bayar was a master warrior and could send his fire everywhere around him in tendrils which were constantly seeking us out. It was all the three of us could do to avoid them. We weren't getting close to the man.

Then there was the constant pressure on our minds. I was guessing it wasn't Kaan but his dragon that was doing it. Keeping us even more on guard. If we slipped up mentally, we'd be dominated again and fight our friends, or perhaps just stop moving to allow Bayar to fry us. So, we couldn't relent in mind or body.

And Pan... by all the spirits, I didn't know how he was still fighting, looking as horrid as he was. He looked like he should be a smoldering wreck, but he fought on just as viciously as Falcon and I.

I have an idea brother, Falcon said to me. *It's stupid, and I may die, but we can finish this dragon lord once and for all!*

Pits no, whatever it is, don't do it, I won't let you die. Dawn and Roo would kill me, and that's if Mother and Father didn't get to me first. There has to be another way.

Sorry, brother, but I don't think there is. I'm going to try to connect with Pan through Dawn and let him know what I'm thinking. Be ready.

Falcon! But even though our spirit-gift inexorably connected us, I knew he wasn't listening anymore. *Blasted, Blackened Bones!* I had no clue what he was planning, which meant I couldn't stop him.

Then trust him, that is all you can do, Isoa said soothingly within me.

He's going to get himself killed!

Perhaps, and if so, then you need to make sure it's not in vain. Or perhaps he'll survive, and we'll win this fight. Let us pray for that.

I gritted my teeth, not liking my choices as I dodged another lashing limb of fire from Bayar. The dragon lord was constantly in motion. We'd been trying to surround him, but he somehow knew where we were. Though, perhaps his dragon was helping. We'd all been surprised by the added blasts of fire from the sky, having to avoid them too. But thankfully, the dragon was also occupied fighting Eophon for the most part. Still, they might have been keeping tabs on us and letting their master know where we were.

I dove under another wave of fire and came up running, headed for Falcon.

But as I reached him, he smiled at me. "Good, you read my mind."

Whatever he was planning I'd played into his hand by going to him; just as he'd known I would.

"What are you going to do?" I hissed.

"No time. Just follow me!"

He charged in at Bayar.

And too late, I figured out what he was doing. I had no choice; I charged in after him. His plan *was* simple and suicidal: he was going to draw Bayar's attention to him and take all the fire the man could pour at him, hopefully blocking me from taking it since I was right behind him. And at the same time, perhaps making an opening for Pan on the other side of the dragon lord.

Falcon, please don't do this!

Ceph can heal me later.

Only if you're not dead!

If I die, what a way to go, what a story. I'll be a legend!

Brother, please!

Then we ran out of time. Bayar turned to Falcon and blasted him with fire. The dragon lord was smiling. He knew if Falcon did dodge the wave of fire, I probably wouldn't be able to. He'd kill one of us.

I don't really plan on dying, brother. I took some inspiration from Dawn...

And as Falcon's body was incinerated, taking the brunt of the firestorm, I felt his spirit slip through our connection into me.

Well... Oh...

Now let's kill him! Falcon urged.

I dove and rolled under another wave of fire, and came up kneeling, finally close enough to Bayar to do something. I slashed with my sword and was rewarded with a scream of pain. I'd hit his leg, cutting through his armor, deep into his calf.

Bayar fell to one knee.

He looked down at me with literal fire billowing out of his eyes and a fist surrounded in flames ready to punch me...

But then a small form landed on his back and knocked him to the ground.

Pan.

I scrambled and slashed wildly, avoiding Pan, but that also meant I wasn't hitting any important part of Bayar. Pan leapt off the man and knocked me back to the ground, protecting me from a surge of fire which burst forth from Bayar in all directions a blast meant to incinerate everything around him. Pan screamed, but I was mostly saved, feeling the heat and taking burns, but nothing too grievous.

Pan rolled off me. "I'm spent, up to you," he wheezed, looking like he'd been double roasted. I was surprised he was still alive.

I launched myself at Bayar as he rose.

He blocked my thrust with the heavy bracer on his arm, knocking my sword aside.

So, I punched him in the face instead. He hadn't been

expecting that, just as I wasn't expecting his skin to be blazing hot, burning my fist.

His head snapped back and for a split second I had an opening. I slashed again, this time for his head. My sword rang off his helm, a glancing blow.

I felt the heat from him and saw his smile. I knew in that instant he was about to explode in flame again. I'd not be able to dive to safety or get out of range, I was a dead man. My only hope was... to slash again and hope I could kill him before he burst with flames.

Time slowed as my sword descended, a back-handed blow, aimed for the small gap between his helm and armor. I saw his skin glow a brighter and brighter shade of red and felt the waves of heat rolling off him. I even saw the fire start to emit from him... then it died instantly, and a look of stunned confusion crossed his face.

But... I hadn't hit him yet.

He's all yours, Roo said into my mind.

Yes! Falcon cheered. *She's taken his fury! Now, brother!*

My sword struck home, driving down into his neck and Bayar went limp as streams of super-heated blood spewed forth from him. Wherever the blood touched me I burned, a final, vindictive curse from the man as he died.

I staggered back and fell to my knees, burned, exhausted and completely drained.

What did you do? I asked Falcon.

What I had to. Ceph and Pan can make me a knew body.

Are you sure, they didn't succeed with Dawn the first time?

It will be easier for us. You're my twin, they don't have to make anything different, they just need to duplicate you. I'm guessing that's a lot easier.

Still...!

Falcon laughed inside me, clearly insane.

I just shook my head. I should see if Ceph and Lyran needed help or... Rhino. I rose, staggering and stumbling. I went to Pan first.

He was still smoking from that last blast of fire, but his eyes opened, and he even smiled up at me. "I'll be well, I'm healing myself slowly. I just need a little rest.

And a lot of bandages.

But I nodded and lurched away toward the others.

And that was when the dragon landed in front of me.

CHAPTER 21

DAWN

"No!" Roo and I shouted as one, seeing the massive beast land in front of Swift. It was Bayar's dragon, enraged at his master's death and about to destroy Swift with fire.

I didn't think, just did what I had to. I blazed forth with spirit, a beacon to any being sensitive to such things. It worked. The dragon swung their head toward me, eyes burning with hatred.

At the same time, I felt Roo pull upon the beast with her powers, trying to drain their emotions, but the feelings of a dragon weren't the same as a human's and it wasn't easy for her to pull upon them. Still, the massive beast seemed to falter for just a moment.

That was all we'd needed.

Swift lunged in, finding a spot where Eophon had torn away skin and scales, driving his sword deep into the creature's chest. At the same time Eophon — also called by my spirit — flew in and clamped an iron jaw around the larger dragon's neck.

The dragon, assaulted from all sides, roared and reared, but it was already too late. Swift plunged his sword in again and again, then Eophon bit deeper, then snapped the other dragon's neck. Swift abandoned his sword and quickly rolled out from under the beast as it died.

Eophon was quickly away to deal with the remaining two dragons.

Swift ran to me. "Thanks."

"You look like the Pits," I said.

Swift smiled, despite his wounds. "I know."

"Don't get yourself killed, there is no place for your spirit and Falcon's to go." My tone was stern.

"And whose fault is that? Not mine!" He grimaced. "But yeah, I'll be careful, I promise, though, I should help the others."

The others...

I didn't know what had befallen Rhino. I sensed his spirit, and through it felt the pain of his body, but at least he was alive. Ceph and Lyran were not far away still battling Kaan. Lyran's older brother was an incredible fighter, still virtually unmarred from fighting both of them, and hardly winded. Whereas Lyran had been torn up badly, only recently healed by Ceph. Now Ceph was also flagging as well.

Swift looked over. "I don't know what I can do... but..." He shrugged. Then he was running off.

Roo had been reaching out as far as she could to the army around us, keeping emotions down, to keep others from arriving like the flood that had overwhelmed Rhino at one point. It was working, but she was quickly growing exhausted. Access to my strength and spirit was helping, but we needed to end this fight quickly.

I would have fought alongside Ceph, Lyran, and Swift, but in Roo's body, I wouldn't be as effective as I would have been in my own.

What can we do? Roo asked. She had tried emotionally draining Kaan, but it seemed his mental powers protected him from other forms of invasion as well. She couldn't affect him. So, instead her efforts had gone into bolstering our guys.

I had thought to tear out his spirit, as I'd done with Swan. But when I'd connected to him, I'd been nearly overwhelmed by his force of spirit, and given how tired Roo's body was, I hadn't been certain I could go toe-to-toe with him in spirit to try to pull his dragon-link out of him. I also didn't know how different that would be than pulling a spirit-gift, like I had with Swan.

"Bones!" I swore. We had to do something.

Rhino came limping out of the darkness. He was missing part of his left leg and looked like he'd been cut up badly, but somehow he was still walking.

He smiled when our gazes met.

"Hey," he said with a grin, then collapsed at my feet. He was still alive, but his body had finally given out on him.

The same was true of Pan, who I knew was not far from where Swift had defeated Bayar. Their bodies were broken even though their spirits were still strong. They wanted to fight, but they couldn't.

Their spirits are still strong! Amya shouted into my mind.

You can use that! Leoa added, catching on.

You're right. I knew what I had to do.

I relinquished control of Roo's body back to her

Keep us alive, I need to concentrate on this! I said and felt her acknowledgement.

I reached out to all our guys and linked with their spirits. And I smiled — even though I had no body to smile with — in that moment. This felt... right.

Falcon, Pan, and Rhino still had strong spirits within them, but were otherwise helpless.

So, I gathered their spirits in this strange swirling void of color. But I also linked with Ceph and Swift. *You two, fall back, but give me all your spirit,* I commanded. There was a certainty in my demand, and they did as asked. I took all their spirits and merged them with my own. Ceph's quirkiness and strange hues, Rhino's strength and earth tones, Pan's dark and mysterious shades, and Falcon and Swift's unity and noble color palette. I took them all in, and made them one within me. Then I pushed all of us into Lyran.

By the Sacred Light! I heard his invigorated wonder.

I gave Lyran Rhino's strength, Pan's toughness, Ceph's

healing, and used the unity of the twins as binding agent to seal the powers into the one man.

We are all one with you now, I said softly. *Do what you must.*

CHAPTER 22

LYRAN

I'D FOUGHT KAAN BEFORE. CONTESTS BETWEEN BROTHERS growing up had been common, but being nearly twenty years Kaan's junior, he had always been bigger, faster, and stronger. Even now, with me in my prime, he was still a far superior swordsman and his moves so efficient that he'd been using far less energy. It was no contest. He'd been solidly thrashing me.

But now...

I felt stronger than I ever had. Was this Rhino's true strength? It was incredible, my speed and strength had increased ten-fold! No longer were Kaan's strikes knocking my sword away when I tried to block. I stopped him, firm.

I saw one of Kaan's brows twitch.

He'd thought, when Ceph and Swift had fallen back, he'd been close to victory, but he knew better now. He was no doubt already scanning the minds of those around us. He'd know what we'd done soon enough.

"Impressive ability," he sneered. "But it still won't be enough." Yet, for the first time ever, I heard just a hint of uncertainty in his tone.

I smiled.

And as I did, I used Ceph's ability to close all the wounds on my body. It drained my energy to do so, but I was more than flush with power at the moment.

I saw Kaan's eyes narrow just a bit, another sign of doubt.

Good.

Then, I went on the offensive. I'd had so few openings in this fight, so now I made one of my own. I saw his blade flashing in toward my side and decided I could take the hit. And if he did hit me, he'd be open to my hit. I put all of Rhino's strength into my slash down at Kaan's head.

He saw it and quickly adjusted his attack, breaking off from his strike to block as he stepped back. And when our swords met, mine cleanly cut through his, sheering it in half. He shifted at the last moment, throwing himself back and I only barely hit him, slicing cleanly through the tip of his nose and the front of his shirt, nothing more.

His eyes went wide. That was the first blood that had been drawn upon him, even if it was a minimal amount.

I pushed my attack.

"I'll just turn your friends against you!" Kaan said, and I saw the twitch of a superior smile. He knew he'd not be able to mentally command me so easily, but the others had already proven susceptible.

And yet... no attack came.

Roo is keeping their emotions low, except for love, which she's surging. Love for all of us. Even if they had thoughts to fight you, they'd not want to. Dawn's voice was certain. *We know how to negate his mental command now.*

I smiled. "You can't turn them against me, not anymore. We are bound by sterner stuff. Try again."

And I saw another crack in the façade of his certainty. He knew my words to be truth. No one was coming to help him. It was just him and me.

Well... him and me and...

Eophon, if Mortagan breaks off the fight with you, kill them while their back is turned.

That is not honorable, Eophon replied. I was glad to hear their voice strong and sure. They were fighting two larger dragons and holding their own. Pan's changes to the dragon had made them more than a match for their consanguines.

Neither is Kaan and Mortagan fighting together against me alone.

True. I will do as you ask... And there goes Mortagan now. They're mine!

"Mortagan isn't coming to help you," I said. "Let's keep this a fair fight, shall we?"

And now, for the first time ever, I saw true fear in Kaan's eyes.

I slashed and hacked at him, and his only recourse

was to give ground and back up. He did try to block another blow with what remained of his sword, and I cleaved through it once again.

He threw what remained of the hilt at me. I dodged it deftly.

"Lyran, brother, you don't want to kill me." His eyes were darting around looking for anything he could use. His hands out to the sides, feigning surrender. I knew he'd never stop fighting me. But he knew I was one heart-beat away from killing him, and he'd do anything to stop that.

"Don't I?" I indulged him, keeping close as he backed off.

"What did I do to you?" he asked. "We raised you, gave you everything. Come back to the empire and..." His eyes went wide as he thought he'd found my weakness. "And you can rule in my place. The empire can be yours!"

I smiled. "With you as my loyal subject?"

"Yes."

I had to laugh. "You'd never truly submit to me. You'd wait till I was in a moment of weakness or not expecting it, then you'd attack. I know you too well, brother."

Kaan's eyes turned hard. He knew he'd lost.

I saw his gaze lingering on something and caught the twitch of his body before he leapt, launching himself at a discarded sword nearby.

I'd seen it too and even as he dove, I threw my sword with every ounce of Rhino's strength. My blade caught him low in the chest while he was in mid-air, just before he landed. The force of the strike knocked him backward. My sword sank to the hilt in his chest, pinning him to the ground.

I walked to him slowly as he coughed up blood. He wasn't dead quite yet.

Weakening arms tried to pluck out my blade but couldn't pull it out.

I knelt next to him as he flailed wild and desperate.

"How does it feel brother?" I said, voice full of bitter irony. "You loved to watch others writhe in the grip of your power, loved to watch them die. Now here you are."

His gaze settled on mine, eyes clearing of pain and desperation for a moment.

"Lyran," he wheezed. "Please!"

He wanted me to save him.

And I did take pity on him. No one deserved a slow death. I drew out a dagger and slashed it across his throat, letting out more blood, then I slammed it down through his skull into his brain.

The life left him instantly.

"Be at peace, brother!"

A dragon screamed somewhere in the distance.

Can you handle them? I asked Eophon. Both the remaining dragons had lost their masters and that could drive a dragon mad.

Indeed. This shall make it easier to defeat them. I will join you soon.

I rose slowly.

I knew she was coming, could feel her acutely

through our linked spirits. I turned and embraced Roo as she threw herself into my arms. "Is it done?" she asked, Roo's tone and cadence, not Dawn's.

"It's done," I breathed.

A new day was beginning, the sky to the east just tinged with light. Soon everyone here would know the dragon lords were dead.

We'd won.

It had cost us another life and far too much pain, but we'd won.

I held Roo tight as I mourned for Falcon. I knew he was with us in spirit, like Dawn, but still...

"I think it's time we got out of here," Ceph said from not far away. He was looking at the ground. "Where was it exactly we were to stomp five times to get that earth-Fey to suck us back down?" With so much destruction, it was impossible to tell where we'd come up. Yet Ceph moved around, stomping the ground five times in various spots, looking just a bit silly.

I laughed, letting out all my pent-up anger and animosity toward my brothers.

Roo turned, watched, then laughed as well.

And we all laughed that much harder when Ceph yelped, sucked down into the ground.

"I guess he found the spot," Roo whispered.

Soon, the rest of us followed.

CHAPTER 23

PAN

Ceph and I were ready to try separating Dawn from Roo again.

The war was over.

After our outing to deal with the dragon lords, the Thraian army had surrendered. Even though they'd still outnumbered us more than ten to one, they'd feared any force that could march into the center of their camp and kill their leaders with impunity. And it had helped that Ensar had gone out to speak to the remaining generals and troops. They would follow him. He had convinced them to return home. And on their way, they'd spread the word that the empire was no more. All lands acquired in the last fifty years or so, would be returned to the people of those lands and funds would be sent to help them rebuild.

Since a majority of the men in the army were from

those more recently conquered lands, they were more than happy to carry the news home.

The queen had been furious with us... then she'd given us all commendations. After that, she'd let us have our time to work on bringing her daughter back to her. We'd all worked on the solution and delved into what had gone wrong the first time.

It had been Dawn herself who had provided the missing link in our planning. The first time, I had failed in recreating Dawn as she should be. I recalled her form, but I hadn't been able to make the cells duplicate her true look. That was because, to my shame, my memory of her was flawed. It had been months since she'd died and though I thought I recalled her well enough, the truth was, I didn't. She wasn't upset at this but proposed that rather than me trying to recreate her from memory, to instead use her spirit, working through me. Her spirit had been connected to her body a lot longer than I'd known her. She'd know all the details.

And Ceph and I had proven that otherwise our efforts would be fruitful. Falcon had been remade, though he and his brother still rested after that ordeal. It had been far easier with them; making a copy, exactly like the first.

After Falcon, we'd rested for several days ourselves. Now, Ceph and I, Dawn and Roo, were all ready.

I floated in a strange place, halfway between the spirit realm of formless colors and reality. Dawn was with me, linked to me, holding me tight and feeling through me to the work I was about to do. Physically my hands were on Roo's hip, where I'd begin my work.

"Ready?" Ceph asked.

I nodded, concentrating too hard to speak.

You'll be well, Dawn said within me. *We will do this together. You'll never be alone again. After this, there will always be a part of me in you, and a part of you in me.*

I love you, Dawn.

I love you too Eadric, Pangolin.

Even though it was far from the first time she'd said those words to me, still my heart swelled to hear them. I'd waited so long to be a part of her life, an intimate part, and now I was. That was a gift I could never repay. But I hoped what I did here today would help.

And I'm here to help as well, Eona piped up. *Take any strength you need from me.*

I will, thank you.

I felt Ceph pushing parts of Roo to me, and I began my work.

And through me, Dawn worked, infusing her spirit — and Amya's — into every bit of the creation process. Her spirit would know what to form and how to form it. And even as we began, growing just a bit of a lump from the side of Roo, I could already see the new skin was extremely pale. It was working.

I smiled, relaxing a little into the work and feeling the warmth of Dawn's spirit with me each step of the way.

It took hours, working slow and steady, to make the body we needed. And this time, though the effort took much from me, I wasn't the sweaty mess of a Fey I had been previously. And as the final moments passed, I wept, seeing the true form of Dawn, perfect and pristine below me.

We ensured Dawn and Amya's spirits were within the form — and Roo and Leoa's were not — then severed the connection between the two linked bodies.

I lifted my hands away, and for a moment, Dawn didn't breathe; she was as still as death.

Then she gasped a great gulp of air and her eyes fluttered open.

She smiled and even though I knew she was extremely fatigued and weak, she forced herself to sit up and embrace me. Roo did the same beside her, embracing Ceph. Finally, we two had our respective women back.

I wept unashamedly, partly from the joy of successfully remaking her, but mostly because the feel of this unique warm body pressed to mine was more than I could bear. I had no words, I couldn't express my gratitude at having her back, so I just cried heavy, happy tears.

"I know," she whispered, voice hoarse, since it had never before been used. "I love you, thank you and you're welcome."

I held her all the tighter until she politely asked me to release her, she needed to rest.

That night, for the first time in months Dawn and Roo slept separately. The other men gave Ceph and I this night, even though we'd be doing nothing but sleeping. I curled close to Dawn and she to me as we rested next to each other. During the night I woke, only to begin crying once again, overwhelmed with joy to have my love back with me. She had died and been remade; a miracle. She was truly special and beyond the confines of this world. And she was mine. Not mine alone, but that didn't matter. I was happy to share her with the others. All together we made the woman ridiculously happy and that was all I wanted for her. And in the moments like this, when it was just the two of us, I could imagine she was mine alone and I was hers alone.

We rested for several days before we both felt recovered enough to be out and about.

There would be a formal presentation of Dawn to her mother, the queen, but before then, one of our first visitors was the queen herself.

CHAPTER 24

DAWN

MY MOTHER CAME TO SEE ME THE DAY AFTER I WAS remade. She hadn't come as the queen, but as my mother, and she was all warm embraces and hot tears, holding me close for a long time.

Pan was still with me, and he gave a breathy, relieved laugh. "I know how you feel, your majesty. Our little miracle has been returned to us."

"Yes, exactly," my mother said through her tears. "And I'll never let you go."

"Never?" I asked. I had always wanted my parents' affection, but I was an adult now and had a life of my own. I may want to venture out into the world again one day.

"I'm so sorry for not being there for you as a child. I know I can't ever make that up. I missed those days and you... you're no longer a child." She was sobbing now. I didn't have Roo's gift, but the two of us were so connected that I could feel the emotions of those around me, if they were particularly strong. My mother radiated remorse and grief, guilt and loss.

It hadn't occurred to me until now that perhaps, not being there for her only child might have taken a toll on her as well. We'd both been scarred by her duties as queen constantly dragging her away. For the first time in my life, I felt sympathy for my mother and held her all the tighter.

She stilled her sobs and spoke again: "I promise I'll be there for you more. It will be easy soon, when I'm no longer the queen."

I pushed away from her, looking her in the eye. "Say that again?"

She laughed through her remaining tears. "There is a lot to tell. Why don't we sit and relax, and I can fill you in?" She wiped her eyes, and I invited her to the small sitting area in my room. Pan and I sat together, our hands clasped between us, and my mother took a chair opposite us. "Actually," she began, "it's all because of you."

"Me?" I asked, stunned.

"Yes. Before you left for Thraan, you'd gotten the notion in my mind of allowing non-True-Bonded into Noble Houses." Oh yes, I recalled that now. One of my better ideas; making the leadership of the nation more diverse. "Well, your father and I — and our little council — discussed this, and we loved the idea. But then we thought... why not just do away with the Nobility and monarchy entirely?"

"What?" I knew my mouth was hanging open, eyes wide.

My mother laughed.

So did Pan. He said, "The Fey rule themselves without kings or queens or nobles; it is possible."

I knew that... but still!

"Just before you returned," my mother continued, "we'd held a vote, of all the people of Elista. We asked if they wished to rule themselves with a government of the people. They said yes. The war side-tracked us, but now we're returning to the process of dismantling the entire Noble system while building a new government."

"Oh..." I breathed. "Wow."

"Yes, it is... quite the task."

"What of Vauphan?" I asked quickly. I knew they'd been fighting my mother and father for pretty much their entire term as queen and king. The Vauphani nobles didn't want to relinquish their power.

The queen grimaced. "That took a lot of work: long nights and hard-fought battles around conference tables. But... their nobles came to see our side of things."

"How?" I asked, curious what my parents had done to finally win-over those stubborn, stuck-up oafs.

There was a specific grin my mother had, which I'd learned was her I've-got-a-cunning-plan grin. She was wearing it now. "We simply explained that if the nobility was gracious and worked with the commoners during this transition, they might retain some of their wealth and power in the new government. If they didn't work with the commoners, well... there are far more commoners than nobles, and Elista would be happy to back a revolution."

My jaw dropped again. "Truly?"

"Truly." My mother was practically beaming. "Your father is there now, working out the details. They are... *happily*... joining with us. Oh, and Basia is going to be a part of this new nation as well, since they lost their monarchs in the war. We'll be one large country, with a capital here in Elista, since that's central to the three. Representatives from all over the three lands will come here to rule this new country, which doesn't even have a name yet."

I shook my head in awe. "Amazing."

"I know, right?" The queen was practically giddy. I could see the young woman she'd been long ago. In that moment, suddenly we didn't feel like mother and daughter, but like... sisters.

Pan kept looking back and forth between us. "I didn't notice it until now, but you two are... very much alike," he whispered.

I would never have admitted that even just a year ago, but now... I did sense how similar we could be.

My mother finished with: "And all of that means I'll have time to finally spend with my daughter; my family." Her expression grew somber. "I'm so sorry for... everything in the past. I was a horrible mother."

"You were," I agreed, then laughed. Then she laughed with me.

"And you," the queen said turning to Pan. "For the time being, I am still queen, with the power of a nation behind me. And you have done a most wonderous thing, returning my daughter to me." She went and knelt before him, taking one of his hands. Pan looked shocked. "Ask anything and it is yours," she said with all solemn seriousness.

"All I want is your daughter," he said softly, heartfelt. My heart melted to hear it. "I... don't know what else I can ask for."

"Think about it, seriously, and whatever you ask, it's yours." She shook her head, then looked from me to him. "I can never repay you for this. Thank you so much, thank you, thank you."

"Now you have to ask for something big," I teased. "Maybe... everything in the royal treasury? Don't ask for land, though. You'd have to keep it up, and pay for tenants, and it's just a pain."

My mother laughed. "I'm going to regret this, aren't I? Still my offer stands. Just don't wait too long or I won't be queen anymore." She rose slowly and embraced Pan, then me.

Her features lit up as she pulled away. "I know one thing I can give you all, you two and the others. Something I never had." She looked back and forth between us. "I loved many, like you, but the world wasn't ready for that sort of a marriage. So, I only married Dawn's father. But..." She shrugged. "Perhaps it's time the world was turned on its head a little. "How would you like to be married?" she said gleefully. "All of you?"

Once again that morning, I found my eyes going wide, mouth falling open.

"That would be amazing, yes," Pan said softly.

"Then it's done! You're all getting married!" And the queen practically skipped out of my chambers.

"Married?" I said slowly.

"It'll certainly be interesting," Pan said. "I wonder how she'll pull it off?" Then he laughed. "Eona seems happy. She's never been married to two women and five other men before. And you know how Lumani love new experiences."

I laughed.

What do you think about this? I asked Amya.

I'm just glad you and your mother are reconciling. The marriage is a symbol, nothing more. I already know you all love each other. This is just making it... official. I'm happy for you Dawn; happy that you're finally happy.

I grinned, a truly peaceful and joyous smile. I *was* happy, perhaps the happiest I'd ever been. And suddenly... I couldn't wait to get married!

CHAPTER 25

ROO

I WORE THE GOLD DRESS I'D WORN TO DINNER WITH THE queen, it was the finest garment I possessed. Everyone said I looked amazing in it, like a golden goddess. So, it seemed fitting to be married in it.

Elista was celebrating and had been for weeks. The war was over, and an entirely new country was being born. So, a full month of festivities had been announced. And this wedding was to be one of the pinnacle events. Held outside in a natural amphitheater with high hills on three sides, this location was usually a place for performers to ply their arts, but today it had been hung with garlands and it seemed like half the nation had been invited to see this curious ceremony.

My sister, Tamia, who was more like a mother to me, had come all the way from our village of Bell Cove and stood with me as my witness. Dawn's witness was — just a bit more prestigious than mine — her mother, the queen. Dawn herself was in a dress of white with subtle highlights of blushing pink, which matched her pale-and-flushed skin. Her black hair was done in special knots over the sides before coming together at her neck and cascading like a waterfall down over her back. My auburn hair was pulled back slightly, but otherwise untended as it fell in waves down over my shoulders and back.

Then... there were our guys.

The twins wore suits, which mirrored each other. One in dark blue with highlights and accents in purple, the other in purple trimmed with dark blue. Their family had come from the East. They were Nobles and had brought all of Tanuki House with them for the celebration, a rather massive extended family of sorts. An interesting counter to Rhino's family, small and humble in their home-spun finery of wool, which suited them, being sheep farmers.

Lyran had no family here. Ensar was already on his way back to the heart of the empire. They'd said their goodbyes formally two weeks ago. Now Lyran was alone, except for this new family we would form. Ceph didn't have much family either. His father was there, an aging man with white hair and a wizened face. Ceph also had a cousin with whom he was close, who had come as well. Then, there was Pan. It seemed like all the Fey had turned out to see him married. The Fey didn't have nobility, but Pan — or Eadric as he was known to them — had been someone important, though the exact nature of his status was lost on me, something to do with his father's skill as a metalsmith? The most notable Fey in attendance was there not for Pan, but for Dawn. Ahmaia was well known to any who'd heard the tales of Queen Legs and her trials before she'd come to power. The Fey woman's dress was of burnished red-gold, and it moved about her elegantly, even though there was no wind this afternoon.

We were married by Dawn's father, King — though not for much longer — Alvere.

Dawn and I were the center of attention, standing together. Her right hand lay upon my left hand, and they had been bound with silken cloth. Even though Dawn and I weren't marrying each other, this symbolized our existing union; we were already bound to each other in spirit. We'd shared a body for long enough to know each other extremely intimately. Even now that we'd been separated, I felt her keenly, and I always would, no matter how far apart we might be. Though something told me, we'd never be too far apart in the future. We were a duo now: two bodies, two souls, but as close as two people could be to being one spirit.

And joining our spirit-union today, would be six others.

Ohhh! I'm so excited! Leoa gushed. *I'm so happy for you, for us, for everyone. I'm just so HAPPY!*

I laughed out loud at her outburst and felt wonderful doing it.

The men came forward, one at a time. Dawn and I

turned slightly to face each other, while Falcon was called. He stepped up and laid his hand on our already bound hands and a different cloth was bound around all three of ours. We said our vows, Dawn and I to Falcon and him to both of us.

"I, Roo, love you, Falcon, and wish to remain with you for all of my life," I said feeling my heart swell as the words of the vow issued forth from me. I had spent some time memorizing them. "We are one: one in body, one in soul, and one in mind." And that was truer than perhaps it would have been for any other couple being married. His spirit was indelibly connected to mine and Dawn's. "We are one with others, who will join our covenant and preserve it. There is no self, only the one life we shall share together. Today, I submit myself to the greater body and soul and spirit which we shall create. No matter the hardships, the sickness or pain, we shall endure. For we shall endure it together, as one. I become we, and we are full of our love."

Falcon smiled, a single tear in one eye as he repeated the vow back to me.

You're stuck with us now, Dawn said through our spirit-link. Falcon and I heard it, and we both smiled, trying not to laugh.

And as Falcon finished his vows, I felt... something. I wasn't sure if it was through my emotion-sense or Dawn's spirit-link or both, but there was a solidifying, a locking of things into place. Our vows had been heard by the spirits and made real. Whatever happened from this day forth, we would truly be one.

I saw Falcon's eyes widen a bit. He'd felt it too.

He kissed me then Dawn, then the wrappings were undone, and Swift came forward to repeat the process, as did all the others in turn.

When Ceph came forward, only he and I said the initial vows. Yet, when we were done, Ceph turned to Dawn and spoke a different vow. "I recognize the twin of my beloved's spirit in you. And though we are not one in body, I will cherish you as I cherish my beloved, for we are one and you and she are one. I will honor and care for you as I care for my beloved and tend to you as I would to her. We are bound by love to our beloved and together shall remain for all our lives."

Pan did the same thing, but in reverse order.

Then... there was a final portion of the ceremony as all of the men returned. They surrounded us laying one hand upon us. Pan was behind Dawn on her left, Lyran behind and to her right. Swift had a hand on her arm, and Falcon next to his brother had his hand on my arm. Behind me were Rhino and Ceph, hands upon my shoulders. Together we recited: "We are one union, bound in love. Let no man nor spirit break us asunder. Our love is stronger for the many of us, and it shall endure beyond life, into the ages. We are one."

A shiver ran up my spine as our voices merged for those final three words. I felt them all within me and myself within them. It was indescribable and perhaps the most beatific and uplifting feeling I'd ever experienced. I saw Dawn's shuddering breath and felt a tremor that began in her and thrummed through all of us.

The crowd roared with cheers and applause, hoots and howls of celebration. This was a new day, and they could feel our love. I knew they felt it, because I was exploding with warmth and affection and may have been leaking it out into the crowd... just a little.

There was a great feast, which went late into the night... but us newlyweds didn't see all of it. We retired to our marriage bed after eating and dancing for a while. We did have to consummate the marriage after all... and what a consummation it was!

CHAPTER 26

DAWN

FIRST, ROO AND I HAD A SHOW. OUR GUYS MADE AN enticing display of stripping themselves. And when their glistening bodies, hard and ready, were revealed in the candlelight, Roo and I went to them. Ever-so-tantalizingly slowly, our dresses were removed. Swift, Pan, and Rhino tended to me, hands gentle, yet insistent as the braids in my hair were unknotted and let down, the ties of the dress were undone, and the silken fabric slowly slipped off me as their lips and hands explored more and more of my revealed skin.

Lyran, Ceph, and Falcon undressed Roo just as slowly, kissing and caressing her full figure. I felt Roo's intense desire; we all did. It radiated off her like she was the sun and it warmed us all.

When my gaze met with Roo's — our gazes both laden with the passion our men were arousing within us — I reached out to her. Her hand raised to meet mine and though we were just out of reach of each other, a spark jumped from my fingers to hers and the power of that response hummed through both of us. Our bodies had been made from one and were known to each other. It was almost like I could feel what she was feeling... No... I actually *was* feeling what she was feeling in that moment. There weren't three sets of lips and hands upon me but six, and the combined sensations of those many loving caresses drove Roo and I to a mutual and very satisfying orgasm even before we were fully undressed.

"Can you...?" she asked. Breath catching with the tremors of her bliss.

"I can," I said. We closed our eyes again and lost ourselves to the sensations of our bodies, both bodies, each feeling what the other felt as kisses and soft strokes, turned into deeper and more heated pressures upon us.

We were lifted and brought to the bed as the wonder of our mutual sensations only grew. We truly were one body now, Roo and I, and when Ceph's lips and tongue upon her folds drove her to the heights of bliss, I too was taken with her. When Falcon's thick cock drove into my pussy as Pan took me from behind, Roo felt it, even as we both felt the combined drive of Ceph and Swift into her. The four cocks drove us mad with pleasure and when we came, Roo made sure everyone felt it. Later, she felt Rhino's soft kisses upon my breast as I felt Lyran's hard raking teeth upon hers. And after a while, I lost track of who was feeling what exactly, as I was propelled to unimagined heights of bliss and wonder, physically and spiritually.

And during one of our rests, over the course of that long and wonderous night, I teased a finger around my oh-so-sensitive nipple, while my other hand traced my folds, and Roo shuddered in delight at the soft sensations. We laughed together at our unity, feeling only the warmth and love that comes with being so closely bound to another, a true friend, a beloved, and one with whom you shared a spirit and the lives of six men.

And when we were thoroughly exhausted, the eight of us snuggled together upon our massive bed. Roo and I faced each other, forehead to forehead, drowsy and content. She giggled then. "You know what this means right?"

"Hmmm?" I said, drifting between wakefulness and sleep.

"Neither of us can be fooling around while the other is trying to do something serious."

That slowly sank into my tranquil mind. My eyes then snapped open. "Oh!" I giggled. "Oh yes, that would be quite... distracting."

I saw her features pull into a suspicious frown. "Which means you're going to do it one of these days, aren't you?"

"Of course." I grinned. "I wouldn't be mischievous little me, if I didn't. I'll have Pan pleasure me until I come like a geyser, and you'll have to keep a straight — if very flushed — face as you meet with some foreign emissary."

She shook her head. "And what if I do the same while you're at dinner with your mother?" Roo asked.

I laughed aloud. "That would be a sight. I might just let that happen to see what my mother would do."

"You're impossible," she huffed.

"And that's why you love me."

"It's why we all love you," Lyran said, kissing my shoulder.

I rolled over to face him. "I'm not feeling so tired anymore, are you?" I whispered.

"Suddenly, no."

"Which means I'm going to be very aroused soon," Roo said behind me. "Rhino, I'm all yours."

We didn't end up sleeping that night.

ALL OF US HAD HAD ENOUGH OF ADVENTURE, DANGER, AND death — at least for a while — and decided to stay in the capital. My mother and father were busy dismantling the monarchy of three countries and amalgamating them into one, and finally, after five months, their work was done. Others were taking over to set up the newly elected government. My parents retired to Hedgewild with Roo and I and our guys as their guests. For the first time in my life, my parents and I truly had time to spend together. My days were spent getting to know them, as adults. It was strange and awkward, but also wonderful and sweet.

And my nights were filled with love.

My plan hadn't been to stay at Hedgewild for a long time. I itched to get back out and see the world. After a half-year in the capital, and a few months here, I was ready to leave again. But by that time, Roo was very pregnant. When I hadn't yet conceived, Pan had a deeper look within me. It turned out I wasn't able to have children, probably because this body was... man-made. I didn't mind at all. Kids hadn't really been on my list of life needs. So, I had the best of both worlds: I'd be a second mother to Roo's children and wouldn't have to suffer through pregnancy myself.

Or so I thought.

As the pregnancy progressed, Roo only grew more radiant and loving and beautiful, of course. And, because our bodies were so connected, I had some changes as well. My breasts swelled, and my body ached a little, uncomfortable at times. Also, I had the strangest cravings. I suddenly wanted pickled fish — and I hadn't even known that was a thing — because Roo did; apparently, she loved it. It was strange to say the least, but I didn't mind. And when the child came, I had the unlucky experience of feeling what Roo felt, so we screamed together until our first daughter was born.

It was clear who little Adora's father was. She had Roo's tawny, honey-gold skin while her indigo eyes were a perfect match for Lyran's.

And we remained at Hedgewild after the child was born. Roo and Adora needed time to recover from the birth.

So, more than a year after the wedding, on a glorious summer's day, I found myself sparring with my mother in the garden.

"You're still dropping your left shoulder," my mother said even as I tapped her arm with the blunt of my sword.

"Yet I still hit you." I stepped back and drew my sword into a salute to signal the end of this match. She did the same.

"Only because of your spirit-gift. You can see how I'll move and what I'll do and that gives you an edge, but it seems that's been trumping your training, your form could still use some work."

She was right, of course, but I didn't like hearing it. I'd survived many battles and thought myself a dominant swordswoman. But I'd come to respect my mother's advice and no longer challenged her at every turn.

I'm so very glad you got to know her, Amya said within me.

Me too.

To my mother, I said, "I'll make sure I have Ceph and the others run me through my paces when we're on the road."

I saw the subtle twitch of her mouth and right eye. I knew it was her concern and fear for me, as well as her love. She'd not say anything about my leaving, but I knew she wanted me to stay longer.

"I'll be back before you know it," I said, dabbing sweat from my face with a towel and putting away my sword. When I turned back to her, she was close and quickly caught me up in a hug. I returned it affectionately. This was a rare display of outright love from her, and I didn't really mind it. She was the one who'd had to shield herself from her emotions as queen for so long. I had no issues letting myself feel how I felt.

"I'll miss you," she said holding me tight. Not 'we'll miss you' or 'your father will miss you' or any of the other phrases she used to say, to distance herself from her own feelings. Perhaps she was finally starting to open up. "I love you, Dawn. I always have." That was a common thing she said these days. It couldn't quite make up for the distance I'd felt from her as a child, but... it was close.

"I love you too, Mom. And don't worry, I have six big guys to protect me and a woman who can squash the fight out of anyone. I'll be well."

"I know, but still, I'll miss you."

"I'll miss you too, Mom."

We shared a bath together, chatting as if we were schoolgirls while we soaked away our aches from sparring. Then Lady Skyfire — who'd come to visit months ago and never left — came in. It was nice when she warmed up the water for us, but then she wouldn't stop talking about herself and we excused ourselves a little later.

I returned to my room and dressed. We wouldn't be leaving today, perhaps not even tomorrow, but some day this week. We were on Roo's schedule now, so I went to see her and little Adora. I heard the baby crying before I arrived in Roo's room.

Do you think...? Amya asked.

Yeah, probably, we'll see.

I entered to find Ceph bouncing and swaying as he walked with the child, trying to get her to settle. I nodded and knew where this was going when everyone in the room — Roo, Ceph, Lyran, and Rhino — all looked at me with expectation.

I sighed. "Okay, give her to Mommy-Dawn," I said, using the cutesy little name Roo used for me.

You know you love this, Amya purred.

Shut up, I do not, I lied. I had to retain my woman-of-action image.

Roo gave a thankful grin as I took our baby. I opened my shirt and brought her to my breast. Because my body had gone through the same transition Roo's had, I was perfectly able to breast-feed little Adora. And it also turned out... Adora simply *loved* to be fed by Mommy-Dawn.

"She's *your* child," I said to Roo, grimacing with the twinge of pain as Adora sought to latch, pulling at my nipple for an awkward moment before settling to feed.

"She's *our* child," Roo said with a sigh, and I could see the slight pain she felt that her baby was so often more comfortable feeding at my breast than hers.

"This will pass," I said, softly, coming to sit next to her. "She'll feed from you more often, I'm sure."

"Tell that to my aching tits," she said and laughed. I laughed with her.

"You have five strapping men who would love to help

you with your aching tits, I'm sure," I countered and laughed at the blushes on all the guys in the room.

And when we'd laughed ourselves out, Roo smiled softly. "I... I am glad you can share in this; that she thinks of you like a mother too. I'm... sorry..."

"Don't be," I said cutting her off, knowing she felt bad about my lack of ability to conceive. "I've told you a hundred times, I am happy with this." I gave her my best grin.

She nodded with a hesitant smile. She wasn't convinced yet, so I went on. "I got all the up-sides and only a few of the downsides of your pregnancy. My tits are bigger than they've ever been, and I have a beautiful daughter. And yeah, it hurt like The Pits to feel you pushing her out, but my pussy is still nice and tight." Though Roo's body had recovered well with help from Ceph, of course. "I may have felt a little achy and awkward for nine-months, but I didn't have to lug around that extra weight, that's the *real* bonus." I smiled at her. "You'll just have to have enough children for both of us."

Roo gave a genuine smile and sighed. "If you say so." Her expression changed to contemplation. "I... have been meaning to ask you about that," she said, clearly growing more hesitant. "I do think I want a large family, but you... want to be out there in the world and exploring. I don't know how compatible those two things will be."

I laughed. "Roo, we have eight of us to care for our children. I think we'll be fine, no matter where we are.

Once we have eight kids and each of us literally has our hands full, then maybe I'll think about settling down."

I'm pretty sure it doesn't work that way, Amya cautioned.

"Eight?" Roo seemed a bit shocked.

"Too many?" I asked. "I thought you wanted a large family."

"Well, yes, but..."

"I guess we'll see," I said, as Adora switched from feeding to sleeping in my arms. I handed her carefully back to Roo, who held her close, adoration in her eyes. The child had been named for the look her mother gave her, every time she held her.

It's the same look you give her, Amya reminded me.

Yeah, I know. Now shut up, I'm not the motherly type.

Riiiiight.

Time to change the subject. "And speaking of leaving," I said, voice hushed now that the baby was sleeping. "How are you feeling?"

Roo looked up at me with a glow about her, a radiant smile on her face. "Eight," she said softly. "Hmm... maybe, yes."

"Did you hear my question?" I asked.

She nodded. "Oh, yes, sorry. Adora and I are both doing well. We can leave anytime."

I smiled. "Tomorrow?"

Roo nodded again, distracted with snuggling Adora. "Yes, tomorrow."

I wasn't really sure if she understood or was just repeating the words. I looked up at Ceph.

"I'll make sure she's ready," he said softly.

"Thanks," I said and covered up before leaving.

Tomorrow it was.

So that evening we said our goodbyes over a long dinner. My Aunt Dove and Uncle Fin were there, visiting. They, like Lady Skyfire, probably wouldn't be leaving any time soon. These Nobles didn't quite know what to do with themselves now that they weren't noble anymore.

And the next morning, bright and early, the eight of us set out. We had a carriage for Roo, who slept most of the morning, having been up and down all-night feeding Adora. Ceph drove the carriage, which also carried all of our luggage. The rest of us were on horseback and were happy to have the wind in our faces once more as we set out.

It was a glorious day and I had everything I wanted and needed. A harem of loving partners, a sister-in-spirit, a renewed relationship with my parents, and the entire world laid before me.

There wasn't anything more I could ask for.

CHAPTER 27

ROO

I HAD THOUGHT TO COME ALONE, BUT MY NEW FAMILY WERE too concerned — and too curious — to leave me be. So, the eight of us crowded around the grave, marked with a small stone, into which were carved the words: Davas, loving husband and son of the sea.

"Wait," Lyran said. "Why didn't I know you'd been married before?"

I smiled over at him. "I thought I'd told all of you, but... that must have been before we met you. Sorry."

He shrugged. "It's not a big thing, just... curious is all."

I nodded, looking back down at the grave, now well covered in grasses and wildflowers. It was odd. I could still recall the touch of his calloused hands, so rough, yet so gentle, and yet... his face seemed to escape my mind. That felt like a loss of something dear, something precious. There was still a hole in my life where he had been, but much of that hole had been filled with the love of my new family. I would never forget my first true love, but I was sure he would be happy for me, having found love again. And there was so much love in my life now. I had my guys, who loved me each in their own way. I had Dawn, who was a part of me; we understood each other like no two women ever had. And... I had Adora, a little bundle of love and the start of our new family.

...with another on the way.

I hadn't told anyone yet. I'd only just discovered it myself a day or two ago.

I was the one who discovered it, Leoa said, tone crisp with mocking reprimand. *And I firmly expect you'll name this next one after me. Leoa works well for a girl, and maybe Leo for a boy?*

You've helped me so much and changed my life in ways I could never have imagined. I think it would be a fitting tribute to name a child after you.

Oh... I was just joking, but... wow... really?

Yes, Leoa, I'll discuss it with the others.

Oh... I think she was shocked to silence after that.

"There is something you should all know," I said rocking Adora softly, still looking at the marker for Davas' resting place.

"You're pregnant again. I know." Dawn sighed. "I can feel the whole thing starting again."

"You are!" Swift said with joy. The other guys chimed in with their congratulations. Ceph and I shared a look while the others rejoiced. He knew it was his. Since Adora had been born, he had been by my side day and night. I'd not slept with any of the other guys in that short time. They could all be with Dawn, but Ceph would only be with me. He had been there for changings and even woken with me for feedings. He'd also comforted me a few times during some rough nights, made the time pass in a more pleasurable way, and it seemed now I was having his child.

And I was delighted to know another was coming. Adora was a blessing and I loved her dearly; more would only add to my joy. I still wasn't sure about the 'eight' Dawn had mentioned, but at least six. I knew I wanted that many. We'd see how things went from there.

"I know you didn't want to leave me alone, but... could I have a moment?" I asked the others.

"Of course," Dawn said. "Shall I take Adora?"

"Yes, please." I handed the sleeping babe over to Mommy-Dawn.

She led the others away, all congratulating Ceph, who still wore a bit of a silly, surprised grin.

I knelt next to the marker for Davas. "I will never forget you," I said softly, stroking the weathered stone. "But I have found a wonderful new life. I wasn't sure I would. I wasn't sure of anything after you died. I didn't know if my life would have purpose again, if I'd have love again, but now I have both. I... I hope you're happy for me. I'm happy for me." I stayed there a moment longer, not sure why I expected some answer on the wind. Nothing came. "I love you, Davas and always will. But you always knew my heart was overflowing. I've found others

I love too, and they love me just as dearly. I... I will never forget you, but I think... finally, I can let you rest in peace. I am well, my love." I kissed my fingers then pressed them to the stone before rising.

For a long moment, I stood on the prominence where the graves of Bell Cove were located. It was a hill overlooking the bay and the village below. I let the wind tousle my hair and skirt, closing my eyes to breathe in the salty sea air. I hadn't realized how much I'd missed that scent.

And soon, I'd be getting much more of it.

Dawn's mother had purchased a sailing ship. It sat out at anchor in the bay, rolling slightly on the waves of the windy day. Tomorrow, it would take us to... somewhere, foreign lands. We didn't really know yet. This was for Dawn, who yearned for adventure, to see every sight there was to see in the world. I had no such desire. Well, I was curious, yes, and I was sure I'd still love to see what was out there, but I didn't need to. I had everything I needed: a sister-in-spirit and a large family, filled with warmth and love.

Tonight, we'd stay with my sister, overcrowding her small house. We'd have a big dinner, if not as extravagant as the one we'd had at Hedgewild. And tomorrow I'd say good-bye to my sister, the woman who had raised me, yet again. The last time, when I'd been Chosen and heading to Silverveil seemed like ages ago. I'd been seeking love and friendship and a lifelong companion. And I'd found all of that. I'd found not just one such person but seven,

even Pan was like a brother to me now. I had found what I sought. My life was full.

I rubbed my belly...

...and it was about to become even fuller.

I smiled, sighed, and made my way down the hill toward the village. The pain and loss of my old life was behind me, and all I carried with me now... was love.

Thank you so much for reading The Shadows Over Elista series! I hope you enjoyed it.

OTHER BOOKS BY CLARA WILS

THE GRECIAN GODDESS TRILOGY

Kiss of the Goddess, book 1

Power of the Goddess, book 2

Bonds of the Goddess, book 3

THE MISTS OF ELISTA TRILOGY

Bonds and Blood, book 1

Shape and Shadows, book 2

Form and Fury, book 3

SHADOWS OVER ELISTA

Double Discover, book 1

Double Danger, book 2

Double Disaster, book 3

Double Doom, book 4

Double Destiny, book 5